Puffin Books
Editor: Kaye Webb

KU-779-288

Penguin Books

With new illustrations
for this edition
by Richard Kennedy

PETER PAN

J. M. Barrie

Penguin Books Ltd, Harmondsworth,
Middlesex, England
Penguin Books Australia Ltd, Ringwood,
Victoria, Australia

First published by Hodder & Stoughton 1911
Published in Puffin Books 1967
Reprinted 1968, 1970 (twice)
Copyright © The Estate of J. M. Barrie, 1911

Made and printed in Great Britain by
Richard Clay (The Chaucer Press) Ltd,
Bungay, Suffolk
Set in Monotype Garamond

Contents

INTRODUCTION – *by Naomi Lewis* 7

Peter Breaks Through 13

The Shadow 25

Come Away, Come Away! 37

The Flight 56

The Island Come True 68

The Little House 84

The Home Under the Ground 96

The Mermaids' Lagoon 107

The Never Bird 123

The Happy Home 128

Wendy's Story 135

The Children are Carried Off 145

Do You Believe in Fairies? 151

The Pirate Ship 166

'Hook or Me this Time' 177

The Return Home 192

When Wendy Grew Up 203

Introduction
by Naomi Lewis

It is a strange fact – yet should it really be a surprise? – that no one can say exactly when *Peter Pan* was born. I do not mean the magic boy, who claimed to be no more than a few days old, but the tale or idea itself. There are hints of someone very like Peter in earlier books and plays by J. M. Barrie, but these were written for adults and all we know for certain of Peter Pan's history is that the familiar play which is still produced each year in the Christmas holidays was first performed on 27 December 1904 at The Duke of York's Theatre in London, and that the full 'story' version was not set down on paper until 1911.

But then everything in the history of *Peter Pan* is, very properly, extraordinary. Except for *Alice*, it must be the most thoroughly English of all invented legends. (Kensington Gardens seem the perfect setting for the Peter Pan statue – you know the one, with animals playing round Peter's feet as he tootles on his pipe.) Yet it was written by a Scotsman who was a grown man before he left the North.

James Matthew Barrie was a weaver's son, born in 1860 at Kirriemuir in Forfarshire (it is on the east side of the map, rather lower down than Aberdeen). He was one of a large family, though not all of them lived to grow up. Even as a little boy he was a tireless reader, and writer too. 'They were all tales of adventure,' he wrote of his own imaginings. 'No characters were allowed within if I knew their like in the flesh. The scene lay in unknown parts, desert islands, enchanted gardens, with knights on black chargers.' In fact, it was all as unlike the bleak local landscape as it could be; later, no doubt, Kensington Gardens, and London houses such as the Darling family lived in must have had for him the same interesting charm of strangeness. The view from the outside, even of our own home, is always the sharpest one.

After leaving school and Edinburgh University (however poor they might be, the Scots never skimped on education) Barrie began to work as a journalist. At the age of twenty-five he took the bold step of moving to London; he first began to make his name by his stories of Scottish life, and later by his plays, among them *Quality Street* and *The Admirable Crichton* – winners to this day, so that by the beginning of the new century the once poor Scottish boy was rich and famous.

Yet when it was finished he felt nervous about offering his theatrical manager, Charles Frohmann, the script of his *Peter Pan*. For it was a child's fantasy, the first and only time he had ever written especially for children. For one thing the director would have to find a way of flying through the air and invent all kinds of strange theatrical devices. However, Frohmann, it is good to relate, was not dismayed but excited. And his excitement was justified. *Peter Pan* was a success from the start, and has gone on being a part of children's lives ever since.

Readers who are interested in how writers work, and how ideas for stories and characters develop, may like to know that the first idea for Peter Pan, the boy who never grew up, appeared in a grown-up novel called *The Little White Bird*. James Barrie had by this time (1902) acquired a special family of child friends, the Davies boys, George, Jack, Peter, Michael and presently baby Nico and the tales and plays that he invented for these children and even the boys themselves began to creep into his 'serious' writings. *The Little White Bird* is about a crusty London bachelor clubman who secretly befriends a penniless young couple, particularly their little boy David. This narrator takes David for walks in Kensington Gardens (as Barrie used to take the Davies boys) and tells him of the mysterious Peter Pan, whose domain the Gardens are at night when the gates are closed. In fact, four years later (in 1906) these chapters were taken out and reprinted as a separate little book called *Peter Pan in Kensington Gardens*, with pictures by Arthur Rackham.

Yes, we recognize Peter in this fascinating story, but the girl in it is not Wendy but Maimie Mannering; and sturdy Maimie, who bravely stays behind at dusk in the closed Gardens though her brother runs away, is a heroine who may appeal to some of us even more than the motherly Wendy. 'You need not be sorry for Wendy,' writes Barrie at the end of the present book. 'She was one of the kind that likes to grow up. In the end she grew up of her own free will a day quicker than other girls.' Even before *The Little White Bird* there are hints, rumours and echoes in Barrie's work of someone very like Peter. In *Sentimental Tommy* the boy of the title imagines a story, a reverie 'about a little boy who was lost. His parents find him in a wood singing joyfully to himself because he thinks he can now be a boy for ever'.

Perhaps, today, the boundary between the child-world and that of the grown-up is harder to trace exactly; often, it seems to have disappeared altogether. But in our grandparents' time, and earlier, the difference between the two states must have seemed truly enormous.

Well, it was a long enough journey from these beginnings to the book that we have now. But whoever persuaded Barrie to write the proper story at last deserves everyone's gratitude. For years, a child who saw the play might think that Peter vanished entirely except for two or three hours in winter; while those who had no chance to see the play knew little about him at all. But the book has also many advantages over the stage production. In the theatre, Peter, and Wendy too, may look confusingly like certain well-known actresses. In the book, Peter stays his own unparalleled self. And the book tells a great deal more. I like to read of Wendy watching the mermaids 'combing out their hair in a lazy way that quite irritated her', or of her scornful feelings when Hook's scurvy hand had tied her to the mast.

No words of mine can tell you how Wendy despised those pirates. To the boys there was at least some glamour in the pirate calling, but all that she saw was that the ship had not been scrubbed for years. There was not a port-hole on the grimy glass of which you might not have written with your finger 'Dirty pig'; and she had already written it several times.

And I like to be told such odds and ends as this: that the island fairies could be good or bad in turn, but never together, since being so small they had room for only one kind of feeling at a time.

As for the opening part about the Darling household, with its terrific climax – nothing of the drama is lost by *reading* that. The parents, you remember, have been warned by Nana, and are hurrying back from the party. They look up at the window.

The room was ablaze with light, and most heart-gripping sight of all, they could see in shadow on the curtain three little figures in night attire circling round and round, not on the floor but in the air.

Not three figures, but four! Will they reach the nursery in time?

In fact the book is so full of surprises, and Barrie is so cunning a story-teller that you don't have to be six years old, or ten, or even twenty, to find this a marvellous piece of reading. Like all the best stories, it offers something to everybody.

'To be born is to be wrecked on an island.' So wrote Barrie in an introduction to Ballantyne's *Coral Island*. A strange idea – but there is a lot of truth in it. We all have to start from the beginning and find what paths we may: what friends, and even foes. In this novel of *Peter Pan* lies one of the most thrilling of all the great adventure islands in fairy-tale; and the account of the children's journey there is as magical as anything in the book. You will notice how it ends:

So with occasional tiffs, but on the whole rollicking, they drew near . . . for after many moons they did reach it, and what is more, they had been going pretty straight all the time . . . because the island was looking out for them. It is only thus that anyone may sight those magic shores.

The island still looks out – it waits, indeed, for anyone venturing into the book that you hold now.

NAOMI LEWIS

This book is part of the J. M. Barrie 'Peter Pan Bequest'. This means that Sir J. M. Barrie's royalty on this book goes to help cure the children who are lying ill in the Great Ormond Street Hospital for Sick Children, London.

1 Peter Breaks Through

All children, except one, grow up. They soon know that they will grow up, and the way Wendy knew was this. One day when she was two years old she was playing in a garden, and she plucked another flower and ran with it to her mother. I suppose she must have looked rather delightful, for Mrs Darling put her hand to her heart and cried, 'Oh, why can't you remain like this for ever!' This was all that passed between them on the subject, but henceforth Wendy knew that she must grow up. You always know after you are two. Two is the beginning of the end.

Of course they lived at 14, and until Wendy came her mother was the chief one. She was a lovely lady, with a romantic mind and such a sweet mocking mouth. Her romantic mind was like the tiny boxes, one within the other, that come from the puzzling East, however many you discover there is always one more; and her sweet mocking mouth had one kiss on it that Wendy could never get, though there it was, perfectly conspicuous in the right-hand corner.

The way Mr Darling won her was this: the many gentlemen who had been boys when she was a girl discovered simultaneously that they loved her, and they all ran to her house to propose to her except Mr Darling, who took a cab and nipped in first, and so he got her. He got all of her, except the innermost box and the kiss. He never knew about the box, and in time he gave up trying for the kiss. Wendy thought Napoleon could have got it, but I can picture him trying, and then going off in a passion, slamming the door.

Mr Darling used to boast to Wendy that her mother not only loved him but respected him. He was one of those deep ones who know about stocks and shares. Of course no one really knows, but he quite seemed to know, and he often said stocks were up and shares were down in a way that would have made any woman respect him.

Mrs Darling was married in white, and at first she kept the books perfectly, almost gleefully, as if it were a game, not so much as a brussels sprout was missing; but by and by whole cauliflowers dropped out, and instead of them there were pictures of babies without faces. She drew them when she should have been totting up. They were Mrs Darling's guesses.

Wendy came first, then John, then Michael.

For a week or two after Wendy came it was doubtful whether they would be able to keep her, as she was another mouth to feed. Mr Darling was frightfully proud of her, but he was very honourable, and he sat on the edge of Mrs Darling's bed, holding her hand and calculating expenses, while she looked at him imploringly.

She wanted to risk it, come what might, but that was not his way; his way was with a pencil and a piece of paper, and if she confused him with suggestions he had to begin at the beginning again.

'Now don't interrupt,' he would beg of her. 'I have one pound seventeen here, and two and six at the office; I can cut off my coffee at the office, say ten shillings, making two nine and six, with your eighteen and three makes three nine seven, with five naught naught in my cheque-book makes eight nine seven – who is that moving? – eight nine seven, dot and carry seven – don't speak, my own – and the pound you lent to that man who came to the door – quiet, child – dot and carry child – there, you've done it! – did I say nine nine seven? yes, I said nine nine seven; the question is, can we try it for a year on nine nine seven?'

'Of course we can, George,' she cried. But she was prejudiced in Wendy's favour, and he was really the grander character of the two.

'Remember mumps,' he warned her almost threateningly and off he went again. 'Mumps one pound, that is what I have put down, but I dare say it will be more like thirty shillings – don't speak – measles one five, German measles half a guinea, makes two fifteen six – don't waggle your finger – whooping-cough, say fifteen shillings' – and so on it went, and it added up differently each time; but at last Wendy just got through, with mumps reduced to twelve six, and the two kinds of measles treated as one.

There was the same excitement over John, and Michael had even a narrower squeak; but both were kept, and soon you might have seen the three of them going in a row to Miss Fulsom's Kindergarten school, accompanied by their nurse.

Mrs Darling loved to have everything just so, and Mr

Darling had a passion for being exactly like his neighbours; so, of course, they had a nurse. As they were poor, owing to the amount of milk the children drank, this nurse was a prim Newfoundland dog, called Nana, who had belonged to no one in particular until the Darlings engaged her. She had always thought children important, however, and the Darlings had become acquainted with her in Kensington Gardens, where she spent most of her spare time peeping into perambulators, and was much hated by careless nursemaids, whom she followed to their homes and complained of to their mistresses. She proved to be quite a treasure of a nurse. How thorough she was at bath-time; and up at any moment of the night if one of her charges made the slightest cry. Of course her kennel was in the nursery. She had a genius for knowing when a cough is a thing to have no patience with and when it needs stocking round your throat. She believed to her last day in old-fashioned remedies like rhubarb leaf, and made sounds of contempt over all this new-fangled talk about germs, and so on. It was a lesson in propriety to see her escorting the children to school, walking sedately by their side when they were well behaved, and butting them back into line if they strayed. On John's footer days she never once forgot his sweater, and she usually carried an umbrella in her mouth in case of rain. There is a room in the basement of Miss Fulsom's school where the nurses wait. They sat on forms, while Nana lay on the floor, but that was the only difference. They affected to ignore her as of an inferior social status to themselves, and she despised their light talk. She resented visits to the nursery from Mrs Darling's friends, but if they did come she first whipped off Michael's pinafore and put him into the one with blue braiding, and smoothed out Wendy and made a dash at John's hair.

No nursery could possibly have been conducted more correctly, and Mr Darling knew it, yet he sometimes wondered uneasily whether the neighbours talked.

He had his position in the city to consider.

Nana also troubled him in another way. He had sometimes a feeling that she did not admire him. 'I know she admires you tremendously, George,' Mrs Darling would assure him, and then she would sign to the children to be specially nice to father. Lovely dances followed, in which the only other servant, Liza, was sometimes allowed to join. Such a midget she looked in her long skirt and maid's cap, though she had sworn, when engaged, that she would never see ten again. The gaiety of those romps! And gayest of all was Mrs Darling, who would pirouette so wildly that all you could see of her was the kiss, and then if you had dashed at her you might have got it. There never was a simpler, happier family until the coming of Peter Pan.

Mrs Darling first heard of Peter when she was tidying up her children's minds. It is the nightly custom of every good mother after her children are asleep to rummage in their minds and put things straight for next morning, repacking into their proper places the many articles that have wandered during the day. If you could keep awake (but of course you can't) you would see your own mother doing this, and you would find it very interesting to watch her. It is quite like tidying up drawers. You would see her on her knees, I expect, lingering humorously over some of your contents, wondering where on earth you had picked this thing up, making discoveries sweet and not so sweet, pressing this to her cheek as if it were as nice as a kitten, and hurriedly stowing that out of sight. When you wake in the morning, the naughtiness and evil passions with which you went to bed have been folded up small and placed at the bottom of your mind;

and on the top, beautifully aired, are spread out your prettier thoughts, ready for you to put on.

I don't know whether you have ever seen a map of a person's mind. Doctors sometimes draw maps of other parts of you, and your own map can become intensely interesting, but catch them trying to draw a map of a child's mind, which is not only confused, but keeps going round all the time. There are zigzag lines on it, just like your temperature on a card, and these are probably roads in the island; for the Neverland is always more or less an island, with astonishing splashes of colour here and there, and coral reefs and rakish-looking craft in the offing, and savages and lonely lairs, and gnomes who are mostly tailors, and caves through which a river runs, and princes with six elder brothers, and a hut fast going to decay, and one very small old lady with a hooked nose. It would be an easy map if that were all; but there is also first day at school, religion, fathers, the round pond, needlework, murders, hangings, verbs that take the dative, chocolate-pudding day, getting into braces, say ninety-nine, threepence for pulling out your tooth yourself, and so on; and either these are part of the island or they are another map showing through, and it is all rather confusing, especially as nothing will stand still.

Of course the Neverlands vary a good deal. John's, for instance, had a lagoon with flamingoes flying over it at which John was shooting, while Michael, who was very small, had a flamingo with lagoons flying over it. John lived in a boat turned upside down on the sands, Michael in a wigwam, Wendy in a house of leaves deftly sewn together. John had no friends, Michael had friends at night, Wendy had a pet wolf forsaken by its parents; but on the whole the Neverlands have a family resemblance, and if they stood still in a row you could say of them that they have each other's nose, and so forth.

On these magic shores children at play are for ever beaching their coracles. We too have been there; we can still hear the sound of the surf, though we shall land no more.

Of all delectable islands the Neverland is the snuggest and most compact; not large and sprawly, you know, with tedious distances between one adventure and another, but nicely crammed. When you play at it by day with the chairs and table-cloth, it is not in the least alarming but in the two minutes before you go to sleep it becomes very nearly real. That is why there are night-lights.

Occasionally in her travels through her children's minds Mrs Darling found things she could not understand, and of these quite the most perplexing was the word Peter. She knew of no Peter, and yet he was here and there in John and Michael's minds, while Wendy's began to be scrawled all over with him. The name stood out in bolder letters than any of the other words, and as Mrs Darling gazed she felt that it had an oddly cocky appearance.

'Yes, he is rather cocky,' Wendy admitted with regret. Her mother had been questioning her.

'But who is he, my pet?'

'He is Peter Pan, you know, mother.'

At first Mrs Darling did not know, but after thinking back into her childhood she just remembered a Peter Pan who was said to live with the fairies. There were odd stories about him; as that when children died he went part of the way with them, so that they should not be frightened. She had believed in him at the time, but now that she was married and full of sense she quite doubted whether there was any such person.

'Besides,' she said to Wendy, 'he would be grown up by this time.'

'Oh no, he isn't grown up,' Wendy assured her confidently, 'and he is just my size.' She meant that he was her size in both mind and body; she didn't know how she knew it, she just knew it.

Mrs Darling consulted Mr Darling, but he smiled pooh-pooh. 'Mark my words,' he said, 'it is some nonsense Nana has been putting into their heads; just the sort of idea a dog would have. Leave it alone, and it will blow over.'

But it would not blow over; and soon the troublesome boy gave Mrs Darling quite a shock.

Children have the strangest adventures without being troubled by them. For instance, they may remember to mention, a week after the event happened, that when they were in the wood they met their dead father and had a game with him. It was in this casual way that Wendy one morning made a disquieting revelation. Some leaves of a tree had been found on the nursery floor, which certainly were not there when the children went to bed, and Mrs Darling was puzzling over them when Wendy said with a tolerant smile:

'I do believe it is that Peter again!'

'Whatever do you mean, Wendy?'

'It is so naughty of him not to wipe,' Wendy said, sighing. She was a tidy child.

She explained in quite a matter-of-fact way that she thought Peter sometimes came to the nursery in the night and sat on the foot of her bed and played on his pipes to her. Unfortunately she never woke, so she didn't know how she knew, she just knew.

'What nonsense you talk, precious. No one can get into the house without knocking.'

'I think he comes in by the window,' she said.

'My love, it is three floors up.'

'Were not the leaves at the foot of the window, mother?'

It was quite true; the leaves had been found very near the window.

Mrs Darling did not know what to think, for it all seemed so natural to Wendy that you could not dismiss it by saying she had been dreaming.

'My child,' the mother cried, 'why did you not tell me of this before?'

'I forgot,' said Wendy lightly. She was in a hurry to get her breakfast.

Oh, surely she must have been dreaming.

But, on the other hand, there were the leaves. Mrs Darling examined them carefully; they were skeleton leaves, but she was sure they did not come from any tree that grew in England. She crawled about the floor, peering at it with a candle for marks of a strange foot. She rattled the poker up the chimney and tapped the walls. She let down a tape from the window to the pavement, and it was a sheer drop of thirty feet, without so much as a spout to climb up by.

Certainly Wendy had been dreaming.

But Wendy had not been dreaming, as the very next

night showed, the night on which the extraordinary adventures of these children may be said to have begun.

On the night we speak of all the children were once more in bed. It happened to be Nana's evening off, and Mrs Darling had bathed and sung to them till one by one they had let go her hand and slid away into the land of sleep.

All were looking so safe and cosy that she smiled at her fears now and sat down tranquilly by the fire to sew.

It was something for Michael, who on his birthday was getting into shirts. The fire was warm, however, and the nursery dimly lit by three night-lights and presently the sewing lay on Mrs Darling's lap. Then her head nodded, oh, so gracefully. She was asleep. Look at the four of them, Wendy and Michael over there, John here, and Mrs Darling by the fire. There should have been a fourth night-light.

While she slept she had a dream. She dreamt that the Neverland had come too near and that a strange boy had broken through from it. He did not alarm her, for she thought she had seen him before in the faces of many women who have no children. Perhaps he is to be found in the faces of some mothers also. But in her dream he had rent the film that obscures the Neverland, and she saw Wendy and John and Michael peeping through the gap.

The dream by itself would have been a trifle, but while she was dreaming the window of the nursery blew open, and a boy did drop on the floor. He was accompanied by a strange light, no bigger than your fist, which darted about the room like a living thing; and I think it must have been this light that wakened Mrs Darling.

She started up with a cry, and saw the boy, and somehow she knew at once that he was Peter Pan. If you or I or Wendy had been there we should have seen that he was very like Mrs Darling's kiss. He was a lovely boy, clad in skeleton leaves and the juices that ooze out of trees; but the most entrancing thing about him was that he had all his first teeth. When he saw she was a grown-up, he gnashed the little pearls at her.

2 The Shadow

Mrs Darling screamed, and, as if in answer to a bell, the door opened, and Nana entered, returned from her evening out. She growled and sprang at the boy, who leapt lightly through the window. Again Mrs Darling screamed, this time in distress for him, for she thought he was killed, and she ran down into the street to look for his little body, but it was not there; and she looked up, and in the black night she could see nothing but what she thought was a shooting star.

She returned to the nursery, and found Nana with something in her mouth, which proved to be the boy's shadow. As he leapt at the window Nana had closed it quickly, too late to catch him, but his shadow had not had time to get out; slam went the window and snapped it off.

You may be sure Mrs Darling examined the shadow carefully, but it was quite the ordinary kind.

Nana had no doubt of what was the best thing to do with this shadow. She hung it out at the window, meaning 'He is sure to come back for it; let us put it where he can get it easily without disturbing the children.'

But unfortunately Mrs Darling could not leave it hanging out at the window; it looked so like the washing and lowered the whole tone of the house. She thought of showing it to Mr Darling, but he was totting up winter great-coats for John and Michael, with a wet towel round his head to keep his brain clear, and it seemed a shame to trouble him; besides, she knew exactly what he would say: 'It all comes of having a dog for a nurse.'

She decided to roll the shadow up and put it away

carefully in a drawer, until a fitting opportunity came for telling her husband. Ah me!

The opportunity came a week later, on that never-to-be-forgotten Friday. Of course it was a Friday.

'I ought to have been specially careful on a Friday,' she used to say afterwards to her husband, while perhaps Nana was on the other side of her, holding her hand.

'No, no,' Mr Darling always said, 'I am responsible for it all. I, George Darling, did it. *Mea culpa, mea culpa.*' He had had a classical education.

They sat thus night after night recalling that fatal Friday, till every detail of it was stamped on their brains and came through on the other side like the faces on a bad coinage.

'If only I had not accepted that invitation to dine at 27,' Mrs Darling said.

'If only I had not poured my medicine into Nana's bowl,' said Mr Darling.

'If only I had pretended to like the medicine,' was
what Nana's wet eyes said.

'My liking for parties, George.'

'My fatal gift of humour, dearest.'

'My touchiness about trifles, dear master and mistress.'

Then one or more of them would break down altogether; Nana at the thought, 'It's true, it's true, they

ought not to have had a dog for a nurse.' Many a time it was Mr Darling who put the handkerchief to Nana's eyes.

'That fiend!' Mr Darling would cry, and Nana's bark was the echo of it, but Mrs Darling never upbraided Peter; there was something in the right-hand corner of her mouth that wanted her not to call Peter names.

They would sit there in the empty nursery, recalling fondly every smallest detail of that dreadful evening. It had begun so uneventfully, so precisely like a hundred other evenings, with Nana putting on the water for Michael's bath and carrying him to it on her back.

'I won't go to bed,' he had shouted, like one who still believed that he had the last word on the subject. 'I won't, I won't. Nana, it isn't six o'clock yet. Oh dear, oh dear, I shan't love you any more, Nana. I tell you I won't be bathed, I won't, I won't!'

Then Mrs Darling had come in, wearing her white evening-gown. She had dressed early because Wendy so loved to see her in her evening-gown, with the necklace

George had given her. She was wearing Wendy's bracelet on her arm; she had asked for the loan of it. Wendy so loved to lend her bracelet to her mother.

She had found her two older children playing at being herself and father on the occasion of Wendy's birth, and John was saying:

'I am happy to inform you, Mrs Darling, that you are now a mother,' in just such a tone as Mr Darling himself may have used on the real occasion.

Wendy had danced with joy, just as the real Mrs Darling must have done.

Then John was born, with the extra pomp that he conceived due to the birth of a male, and Michael came from his bath to ask to be born also, but John said brutally that they did not want any more.

Michael had nearly cried. 'Nobody wants me,' he said, and of course the lady in evening-dress could not stand that.

'I do,' she said. 'I so want a third child.'

'Boy or girl?' asked Michael, not too hopefully.

'Boy.'

Then he had leapt into her arms. Such a little thing for Mr and Mrs Darling and Nana to recall now, but not so little if that was to be Michael's last night in that nursery.

They go on with their recollections.

'It was then that I rushed in like a tornado, wasn't it?' Mr Darling would say, scorning himself; and indeed he had been like a tornado.

Perhaps there was some excuse for him. He, too, had been dressing for the party, and all had gone well with him until he came to his tie. It is an astounding thing to have to tell, but this man, though he knew about stocks and shares, had no real mastery of his tie. Sometimes the thing yielded to him without a contest, but there were occasions when it would have been better for the house if he had swallowed his pride and used a made-up tie!

This was such an occasion. He came rushing into the nursery with the crumpled little brute of a tie in his hand.

'Why, what is the matter, father, dear?'

'Matter!' he yelled; he really yelled. 'This tie, it will not tie.' He became dangerously sarcastic. 'Not round my neck! Round the bedpost! Oh yes, twenty times have I made it up round the bedpost, but round my neck, no! Oh dear no! begs to be excused!'

He thought Mrs Darling was not sufficiently impressed, and he went on sternly, 'I warn you of this, mother, that unless this tie is round my neck we don't go out to dinner tonight, and if I don't go out to dinner tonight, I never go to the office again, and if I don't go to the office again, you and I starve, and our children will be flung into the streets.'

Even then Mrs Darling was placid. 'Let me try, dear,' she said, and indeed that was what he had come to ask her to do; and with her nice cool hands she tied his tie for him, while the children stood around to see their fate decided. Some men would have resented her being able to do it so easily, but Mr Darling was far too fine a nature for that; he thanked her carelessly, at once forgot his rage, and in another moment was dancing round the room with Michael on his back.

'How wildly we romped!' said Mrs Darling now, recalling it.

'Our last romp!' Mr Darling groaned.

'Oh George, do you remember Michael suddenly said to me, "How did you get to know me, mother?"'

'I remember!'

'They were rather sweet, don't you think, George?'

'And they were ours, ours, and now they are gone.'

The romp had ended with the appearance of Nana, and

most unluckily Mr Darling collided against her, covering his trousers with hairs. They were not only new trousers but they were the first he had ever had with braid on them, and he had to bite his lip to prevent the tears coming. Of course Mrs Darling brushed him, but he began to talk again about its being a mistake to have a dog for a nurse.

'George, Nana is a treasure.'

'No doubt, but I have an uneasy feeling at times that she looks upon the children as puppies.'

'Oh no, dear one, I feel sure she knows they have souls.'

'I wonder,' Mr Darling said thoughtfully, 'I wonder.' It was an opportunity, his wife felt, for telling him about the boy. At first he pooh-poohed the story, but he became thoughtful when she showed him the shadow.

'It is nobody I know,' he said, examining it carefully, 'but he does look a scoundrel.'

'We were still discussing it, you remember,' says Mr Darling, 'when Nana came in with Michael's medicine. You will never carry the bottle in your mouth again, Nana, and it is all my fault.'

Strong man though he was, there is no doubt that he had behaved rather foolishly over the medicine. If he had a weakness, it was for thinking that all his life he had taken medicine boldly; and so now, when Michael dodged the spoon in Nana's mouth, he had said reprovingly, 'Be a man, Michael.'

'Won't; won't,' Michael cried naughtily. Mrs Darling left the room to get a chocolate for him, and Mr Darling thought this showed want of firmness.

'Mother, don't pamper him,' he called after her. 'Michael, when I was your age I took medicine without a murmur. I said "Thank you, kind parents, for giving me bottles to make me well."'

He really thought this was true, and Wendy, who was

now in her night-gown, believed it also, and she said, to encourage Michael, 'That medicine you sometimes take, father, is much nastier, isn't it?'

'Ever so much nastier,' Mr Darling said bravely, 'and I would take it now as an example to you, Michael, if I hadn't lost the bottle.'

He had not exactly lost it; he had climbed in the dead of night to the top of the wardrobe and hidden it there. What he did not know was that the faithful Liza had found it, and put it back on his wash-stand.

'I know where it is, father,' Wendy cried, always glad to be of service. 'I'll bring it,' and she was off before he could stop her. Immediately his spirits sank in the strangest way.

'John,' he said, shuddering, 'it's most beastly stuff. It's that nasty, sticky, sweet kind.'

'It will soon be over, father,' John said cheerily, and then in rushed Wendy with the medicine in a glass.

'I have been as quick as I could,' she panted.

'You have been wonderfully quick,' her father retorted, with a vindictive politeness that was quite thrown away upon her. 'Michael first,' he said doggedly.

'Father first,' said Michael, who was of a suspicious nature.

'I shall be sick, you know,' Mr Darling said threateningly.

'Come on, father,' said John.

'Hold your tongue, John,' his father rapped out.

Wendy was quite puzzled. 'I thought you took it quite easily, father.'

'That is not the point,' he retorted. 'The point is, that there is more in my glass than in Michael's spoon.' His proud heart was nearly bursting. 'And it isn't fair; I would say it though it were with my last breath – it isn't fair.'

'Father, I am waiting,' said Michael coldly.

'It's all very well to say you are waiting; so am I waiting.'

'Father's a cowardy custard.'

'So are you a cowardy custard.'

'I'm not frightened.'

'Neither am I frightened.'

'Well, then, take it.'

'Well, then, you take it.'

Wendy had a splendid idea. 'Why not both take it at the same time?'

'Certainly,' said Mr Darling. 'Are you ready, Michael?'

Wendy gave the words, one, two, three, and Michael took his medicine, but Mr Darling slipped his behind his back.

There was a yell of rage from Michael, and 'O father!' Wendy exclaimed.

'What do you mean by "O father"?' Mr Darling demanded. 'Stop that row, Michael. I meant to take mine, but I – I missed it.'

It was dreadful the way all the three were looking at him, just as if they did not admire him. 'Look here, all of you,' he said entreatingly, as soon as Nana had gone into the bathroom, 'I have just thought of a splendid joke. I shall pour my medicine into Nana's bowl, and she will drink it, thinking it is milk!'

It was the colour of milk; but the children did not have their father's sense of humour, and they looked at him reproachfully as he poured the medicine into Nana's bowl. 'What fun,' he said doubtfully, and they did not dare expose him when Mrs Darling and Nana returned.

'Nana, good dog,' he said, patting her, 'I have put a little milk into your bowl, Nana.'

Nana wagged her tail, ran to the medicine, and began lapping it. Then she gave Mr Darling such a look, not an angry look: she showed him the great red tear that makes us so sorry for noble dogs, and crept into her kennel.

Mr Darling was frightfully ashamed of himself, but he would not give in. In a horrid silence Mrs Darling smelt the bowl. 'O George,' she said, 'it's your medicine!'

'It was only a joke,' he roared, while she comforted her boys, and Wendy hugged Nana. 'Much good,' he said bitterly, 'my wearing myself to the bone trying to be funny in this house.'

And still Wendy hugged Nana. 'That's right,' he shouted. 'Coddle her! Nobody coddles me. Oh dear no! I am only the breadwinner, why should I be coddled, why, why, why!'

'George,' Mrs Darling entreated him, 'not so loud; the servants will hear you.' Somehow they had got into the way of calling Liza the servants.

'Let them,' he answered recklessly. 'Bring in the whole world. But I refuse to allow that dog to lord it in my nursery for an hour longer.'

The children wept, and Nana ran to him beseechingly, but he waved her back. He felt he was a strong man again. 'In vain, in vain,' he cried; 'the proper place for you is the yard, and there you go to be tied up this instant.'

'George, George,' Mrs Darling whispered, 'remember what I told you about that boy.'

Alas, he would not listen. He was determined to show who was master in that house, and when commands would not draw Nana from the kennel, he lured her out of it with honeyed words, and seizing her roughly, dragged her from the nursery. He was ashamed of himself, and yet he did it. It was all owing to his too affectionate nature, which craved for admiration. When he had tied her up in the backyard, the wretched father went and sat in the passage, with his knuckles to his eyes.

In the meantime Mrs Darling had put the children to bed in unwonted silence and lit their night-lights. They could hear Nana barking, and John whimpered, 'It is because he is chaining her up in the yard,' but Wendy was wiser.

'That is not Nana's unhappy bark,' she said, little guessing what was about to happen; 'that is her bark when she smells danger.'

Danger!

'Are you sure, Wendy?'

'Oh yes.'

Mrs Darling quivered and went to the window. It was securely fastened. She looked out, and the night was peppered with stars. They were crowding round the house, as if curious to see what was to take place there, but she did not notice this, nor that one or two of the smaller ones winked at her. Yet a nameless fear clutched at her heart and made her cry, 'Oh, how I wish that I wasn't going to a party tonight!'

Even Michael, already half asleep, knew that she was perturbed, and he asked, 'Can anything harm us, mother, after the night-lights are lit?'

'Nothing, precious,' she said; 'they are the eyes a mother leaves behind her to guard her children.'

She went from bed to bed singing enchantments over them, and little Michael flung his arms round her. 'Mother,' he cried, 'I'm glad of you.' They were the last words she was to hear from him for a long time.

No. 27 was only a few yards distant, but there had been a slight fall of snow, and Father and Mother Darling picked their way over it deftly not to soil their shoes. They were already the only persons in the street, and all the stars were watching them. Stars are beautiful, but they may not take an active part in anything, they must just look on for ever. It is a punishment put on them for something they did so long ago that no star now knows what it was. So the older ones have become glassy-eyed and seldom speak (winking is the star language), but the little ones still wonder. They are not really friendly to Peter, who has a mischievous way of stealing up behind them and trying to blow them out; but they are so fond of fun that they were on his side tonight, and anxious to get the grown-ups out of the way. So as soon as the door of 27 closed on Mr and Mrs Darling there was a commotion in the firmament, and the smallest of all the stars in the Milky Way screamed out:

'Now, Peter!'

3 Come Away, Come Away!

For a moment after Mr and Mrs Darling left the house the night-lights by the beds of the three children continued to burn clearly. They were awfully nice little night-lights, and one cannot help wishing that they could have kept awake to see Peter; but Wendy's light blinked and gave such a yawn that the other two yawned also, and before they could close their mouths all the three went out.

There was another light in the room now, a thousand times brighter than the night-lights, and in the time we have taken to say this, it has been in all the drawers in the nursery, looking for Peter's shadow, rummaged the wardrobe and turned every pocket inside out. It was not really a light; it made this light by flashing about so quickly, but when it came to rest for a second you saw it was a fairy, no longer than your hand, but still growing. It was a girl called Tinker Bell, exquisitely gowned in a skeleton leaf, cut low and square, through which her figure could be seen to the best advantage. She was slightly inclined to *embonpoint*.

A moment after the fairy's entrance the window was blown open by the breathing of the little stars, and Peter dropped in. He had carried Tinker Bell part of the way, and his hand was still messy with the fairy dust.

'Tinker Bell,' he called softly, after making sure that the children were asleep, 'Tink, where are you?' She was in a jug for the moment, and liking it extremely; she had never been in a jug before.

'Oh, do come out of that jug, and tell me, do you know where they put my shadow?'

The loveliest tinkle as of golden bells answered him. It is the fairy language. You ordinary children can never hear it, but if you were to hear it you would know that you had heard it once before.

Tink said that the shadow was in the big box. She meant the chest of drawers, and Peter jumped at the drawers, scattering their contents to the floor with both hands, as kings toss ha'pence to the crowd. In a moment he had recovered his shadow, and in his delight he forgot that he had shut Tinker Bell up in the drawer.

If he thought at all, but I don't believe he ever thought, it was that he and his shadow, when brought near each other, would join like drops of water; and when they did not he was appalled. He tried to stick it on with soap from the bathroom, but that also failed. A shudder passed through Peter, and he sat on the floor and cried.

His sobs woke Wendy, and she sat up in bed. She was not alarmed to see a stranger crying on the nursery floor; she was only pleasantly interested.

'Boy,' she said courteously, 'why are you crying?'

Peter could be exceedingly polite also, having learned the grand manner at fairy ceremonies, and he rose and bowed to her beautifully. She was much pleased, and bowed beautifully to him from the bed.

'What's your name?' he asked.

'Wendy Moira Angela Darling,' she replied with some satisfaction. 'What is your name?'

'Peter Pan.'

She was already sure that he must be Peter, but it did seem a comparatively short name.

'Is that all?'

'Yes,' he said rather sharply. He felt for the first time that it was a shortish name.

'I'm so sorry,' said Wendy Moira Angela.

'It doesn't matter,' Peter gulped.

She asked where he lived.

'Second to the right,' said Peter, 'and then straight on till morning.'

'What a funny address!'

Peter had a sinking. For the first time he felt that perhaps it was a funny address.

'No, it isn't,' he said.

'I mean,' Wendy said nicely, remembering that she was hostess, 'is that what they put on the letters?'

He wished she had not mentioned letters.

'Don't get any letters,' he said contemptuously.

'But your mother gets letters?'

'Don't have a mother,' he said. Not only had he no mother, but he had not the slightest desire to have one. He thought them very over-rated persons. Wendy, however, felt at once that she was in the presence of a tragedy.

'O Peter, no wonder you were crying,' she said, and got out of bed and ran to him.

'I wasn't crying about mothers,' he said rather indignantly. 'I was crying because I can't get my shadow to stick on. Besides, I wasn't crying.'

'It has come off?'

'Yes.'

Then Wendy saw the shadow on the floor, looking so draggled, and she was frightfully sorry for Peter. 'How awful!' she said, but she could not help smiling when she saw that he had been trying to stick it on with soap. How exactly like a boy!

Fortunately she knew at once what to do. 'It must be sewn on,' she said, just a little patronizingly.

'What's sewn?' he asked.

'You're dreadfully ignorant.'

'No, I'm not.'

But she was exulting in his ignorance. 'I shall sew it on for you, my little man,' she said, though he was as tall as herself; and she got out her housewife, and sewed the shadow on to Peter's foot.

'I dare say it will hurt a little,' she warned him.

'Oh, I shan't cry,' said Peter, who was already of opinion that he had never cried in his life. And he clenched his teeth and did not cry; and soon his shadow was behaving properly, though still a little creased.

'Perhaps I should have ironed it,' Wendy said thoughtfully; but Peter, boylike, was indifferent to appearances, and he was now jumping about in the wildest glee. Alas, he had already forgotten that he owed his bliss to Wendy. He thought he had attached the shadow himself. 'How clever I am,' he crowed rapturously, 'oh, the cleverness of me!'

It is humiliating to have to confess that this conceit of Peter was one of his most fascinating qualities. To put it with brutal frankness, there never was a cockier boy.

But for the moment Wendy was shocked. 'Your conceit,' she exclaimed with frightful sarcasm; 'of course I did nothing!'

'You did a little,' Peter said carelessly, and continued to dance.

'A little!' she replied with hauteur; 'if I am no use I can at least withdraw'; and she sprang in the most

dignified way into bed and covered her face with the
blankets.

To induce her to look up he pretended to be going
away, and when this failed he sat on the end of the bed
and tapped her gently with his foot. 'Wendy,' he said,
'don't withdraw. I can't help crowing, Wendy, when
I'm pleased with myself.' Still she would not look up,
though she was listening eagerly. 'Wendy,' he continued in a voice that no woman has ever yet been able
to resist, 'Wendy, one girl is more use than twenty
boys.'

Now Wendy was every inch a woman, though there
were not very many inches, and she peeped out of the
bedclothes.

'Do you really think so, Peter?'

'Yes, I do.'

'I think it's perfectly sweet of you,' she declared, 'and
I'll get up again'; and she sat with him on the side of the
bed. She also said she would give him a kiss if he liked,

but Peter did not know what she meant, and he held out his hand expectantly.

'Surely you know what a kiss is?' she asked, aghast.

'I shall know when you give it to me,' he replied stiffly; and not to hurt his feelings she gave him a thimble.

'Now,' said he, 'shall I give you a kiss?' and she replied with a slight primness, 'If you please.' She made herself rather cheap by inclining her face towards him, but he merely dropped an acorn button into her hand; so she slowly returned her face to where it had been before, and said nicely that she would wear his kiss on the chain round her neck. It was lucky that she did put it on that chain, for it was afterwards to save her life.

When people in our set are introduced, it is customary for them to ask each other's age, and so Wendy, who always liked to do the correct thing, asked Peter how old he was. It was not really a happy question to ask him; it was like an examination paper that asks grammar, when what you want to be asked is Kings of England.

'I don't know,' he replied uneasily, 'but I am quite young.' He really knew nothing about it; he had merely suspicions, but he said at a venture, 'Wendy, I ran away the day I was born.'

Wendy was quite surprised, but interested; and she indicated in the charming drawing-room manner, by a touch on her night-gown, that he could sit nearer her.

'It was because I heard father and mother,' he explained in a low voice, 'talking about what I was to be when I became a man.' He was extraordinarily agitated now. 'I don't want ever to be a man,' he said with passion. 'I want always to be a little boy and to have fun. So I ran away to Kensington Gardens and lived a long long time among the fairies.'

She gave him a look of the most intense admiration, and he thought it was because he had run away, but it was really because he knew fairies. Wendy had lived such a home life that to know fairies struck her as quite delightful. She poured out questions about them, to his surprise, for they were rather a nuisance to him, getting in his way and so on, and indeed he sometimes had to give them a hiding. Still, he liked them on the whole, and he told her about the beginning of fairies.

'You see, Wendy, when the first baby laughed for the first time, its laugh broke into a thousand pieces, and they all went skipping about, and that was the beginning of fairies.'

Tedious talk this, but being a stay-at-home she liked it.

'And so,' he went on good-naturedly, 'there ought to be one fairy for every boy and girl.'

'Ought to be? Isn't there?'

'No. You see, children know such a lot now, they soon don't believe in fairies, and every time a child says, "I don't believe in fairies," there is a fairy somewhere that falls down dead.'

Really, he thought they had now talked enough about fairies, and it struck him that Tinker Bell was keeping very quiet. 'I can't think where she has gone to,' he said, rising, and he called Tink by name. Wendy's heart went flutter with a sudden thrill.

'Peter,' she cried, clutching him, 'you don't mean to tell me that there is a fairy in this room!'

'She was here just now,' he said a little impatiently. 'You don't hear her, do you?' and they both listened.

'The only sound I hear,' said Wendy, 'is like a tinkle of bells.'

'Well, that's Tink, that's the fairy language. I think I hear her too.'

The sound came from the chest of drawers, and Peter made a merry face. No one could ever look quite so merry as Peter, and the loveliest of gurgles was his laugh. He had his first laugh still.

'Wendy,' he whispered gleefully, 'I do believe I shut her up in the drawer!'

He let poor Tink out of the drawer, and she flew about the nursery screaming with fury. 'You shouldn't say such things,' Peter retorted. 'Of course I'm very sorry, but how could I know you were in the drawer?'

Wendy was not listening to him. 'O Peter,' she cried, 'if she would only stand still and let me see her!'

'They hardly ever stand still,' he said, but for one moment Wendy saw the romantic figure come to rest on the cuckoo clock. 'O the lovely!' she cried, though Tink's face was still distorted with passion.

'Tink,' said Peter amiably, 'this lady says she wishes you were her fairy.'

Tinker Bell answered insolently.

'What does she say, Peter?'

He had to translate. 'She is not very polite. She says you are a great ugly girl, and that she is my fairy.'

He tried to argue with Tink. 'You know you can't be my fairy, Tink, because I am a gentleman and you are a lady.'

To this Tink replied in these words, 'You silly ass,' and disappeared into the bathroom. 'She is quite a common fairy,' Peter explained apologetically; 'she is called Tinker Bell because she mends the pots and kettles.'

They were together in the arm-chair by this time, and Wendy plied him with more questions.

'If you don't live in Kensington Gardens now –'

'Sometimes I do still.'

'But where do you live mostly now?'

'With the lost boys.'

'Who are they?'

'They are the children who fall out of their perambulators when the nurse is looking the other way. If they are not claimed in seven days they are sent far away to the Neverland to defray expenses. I'm captain.'

'What fun it must be!'

'Yes,' said cunning Peter, 'but we are rather lonely. You see we have no female companionship.'

'Are none of the others girls?'

'Oh no; girls, you know, are much too clever to fall out of their prams.'

This flattered Wendy immensely. 'I think,' she said, 'it is perfectly lovely the way you talk about girls; John there just despises us.'

For reply Peter rose and kicked John out of bed, blankets and all; one kick. This seemed to Wendy rather forward for a first meeting, and she told him with spirit that he was not captain in her house. However, John continued to sleep so placidly on the floor that she allowed him to remain there. 'And I know you meant to be kind,' she said, relenting, 'so you may give me a kiss.'

For a moment she had forgotten his ignorance about kisses. 'I thought you would want it back,' he said a little bitterly, and offered to return her the thimble.

'Oh dear,' said the nice Wendy, 'I don't mean a kiss, I mean a thimble.'

'What's that?'

'It's like this.' She kissed him.

'Funny!' said Peter gravely. 'Now shall I give you a thimble?'

'If you wish to,' said Wendy, keeping her head erect this time.

Peter thimbled her, and almost immediately she screeched. 'What is it, Wendy?'

'It was exactly as if someone were pulling my hair.'

'That must have been Tink. I never knew her so naughty before.'

And indeed Tink was darting about again, using offensive language.

'She says she will do that to you, Wendy, every time I give you a thimble.'

'But why?'

'Why, Tink?'

Again Tink replied, 'You silly ass.' Peter could not understand why, but Wendy understood; and she was just slightly disappointed when he admitted that he came to the nursery window not to see her but to listen to stories.

'You see I don't know any stories. None of the lost boys know any stories.'

'How perfectly awful,' Wendy said.

'Do you know,' Peter asked, 'why swallows build in the eaves of houses? It is to listen to the stories. O Wendy, your mother was telling you such a lovely story.'

'Which story was it?'

'About the prince who couldn't find the lady who wore the glass slipper.'

'Peter,' said Wendy excitedly, 'that was Cinderella, and he found her, and they lived happy ever after.'

Peter was so glad that he rose from the floor, where they had been sitting, and hurried to the window. 'Where are you going?' she cried with misgiving.

'To tell the other boys.'

'Don't go, Peter,' she entreated, 'I know such lots of stories.'

Those were her precise words, so there can be no denying that it was she who first tempted him.

He came back, and there was a greedy look in his eyes now which ought to have alarmed her, but did not.

'Oh, the stories I could tell to the boys!' she cried, and then Peter gripped her and began to draw her towards the window.

'Let me go!' she ordered him.

'Wendy, do come with me and tell the other boys.'

Of course she was very pleased to be asked, but she said, 'Oh dear, I can't. Think of mummy! Besides, I can't fly.'

'I'll teach you.'

'Oh, how lovely to fly.'

'I'll teach you how to jump on the wind's back, and then away we go.'

'Oo!' she exclaimed rapturously.

'Wendy, Wendy, when you are sleeping in your silly bed you might be flying about with me saying funny things to the stars.'

'Oo!'

'And, Wendy, there are mermaids.'

'Mermaids! With tails?'

'Such long tails.'

'Oh,' cried Wendy, 'to see a mermaid!'

He had become frightfully cunning. 'Wendy,' he said, 'how we should all respect you.'

She was wriggling her body in distress. It was quite as if she were trying to remain on the nursery floor.

But he had no pity for her.

'Wendy,' he said, the sly one, 'you could tuck us in at night.'

'Oo!'

'None of us has ever been tucked in at night.'

'Oo,' and her arms went out to him.

'And you could darn our clothes, and make pockets for us. None of us has any pockets.'

How could she resist? 'Of course it's awfully fascinating!' she cried. 'Peter, would you teach John and Michael to fly too?'

'If you like,' he said indifferently; and she ran to John and Michael and shook them. 'Wake up,' she cried, 'Peter Pan has come and he is to teach us to fly.'

John rubbed his eyes. 'Then I shall get up,' he said. Of course he was on the floor already. 'Hallo,' he said, 'I am up!'

Michael was up by this time also, looking as sharp as a knife with six blades and a saw, but Peter suddenly signed silence. Their faces assumed the awful craftiness of children listening for sounds from the grown-up world. All was as still as salt. Then everything was right. No, stop! Everything was wrong. Nana, who had been barking distressfully all the evening, was quiet now. It was her silence they had heard.

'Out with the light! Hide! Quick!' cried John, taking command for the only time throughout the whole adventure. And thus when Liza entered, holding Nana, the nursery seemed quite its old self, very dark; and you could have sworn you heard its three wicked inmates breathing angelically as they slept. They were really doing it artfully from behind the window curtains.

Liza was in a bad temper, for she was mixing the Christmas puddings in the kitchen, and had been drawn away from them, with a raisin still on her cheek, by Nana's absurd suspicions. She thought the best way of getting a little quiet was to take Nana to the nursery for a moment, but in custody of course.

'There, you suspicious brute,' she said, not sorry that Nana was in disgrace, 'they are perfectly safe, aren't they? Every one of the little angels sound asleep in bed. Listen to their gentle breathing.'

Here Michael, encouraged by his success, breathed so loudly that they were nearly detected. Nana knew that kind of breathing, and she tried to drag herself out of Liza's clutches.

But Liza was dense. 'No more of it, Nana,' she said sternly, pulling her out of the room. 'I warn you if you bark again I shall go straight for master and missus and bring them home from the party, and then, oh, won't master whip you, just.'

She tied the unhappy dog up again, but do you think Nana ceased to bark? Bring master and missus home from the party! Why, that was just what she wanted. Do you think she cared whether she was whipped so long as her charges were safe? Unfortunately Liza returned to her puddings, and Nana, seeing that no help would come from her, strained and strained at the chain until at last she broke it. In another moment she had burst into the dining room of 27 and flung up her paws to heaven, her most expressive way of making a communication. Mr and Mrs Darling knew at once that something terrible was happening in their nursery, and without a good-bye to their hostess they rushed into the street.

But it was now ten minutes since three scoundrels had been breathing behind the curtains; and Peter Pan can do a great deal in ten minutes.

We now return to the nursery.

'It's all right,' John announced, emerging from his hiding-place. 'I say, Peter, can you really fly?'

Instead of troubling to answer him Peter flew round the room, taking in the mantelpiece on the way.

'How topping!' said John and Michael.

'How sweet!' cried Wendy.

'Yes, I'm sweet, oh, I am sweet!' said Peter, forgetting his manners again.

It looked delightfully easy, and they tried it first from the floor and then from the beds, but they always went down instead of up.

'I say, how do you do it?' asked John, rubbing his knee. He was quite a practical boy.

'You just think lovely wonderful thoughts,' Peter explained, 'and they lift you up in the air.'

He showed them again.

'You're so nippy at it,' John said; 'couldn't you do it very slowly once?'

Peter did it both slowly and quickly. 'I've got it now, Wendy!' cried John, but soon he found he had not. Not one of them could fly an inch, though even Michael was in words of two syllables, and Peter did not know A from Z.

Of course Peter had been trifling with them, for no one can fly unless the fairy dust has been blown on him. Fortunately, as we have mentioned, one of his hands was messy with it, and he blew some on each of them, with the most superb results.

'Now just wriggle your shoulders this way,' he said, 'and let go.'

They were all on their beds, and gallant Michael let go first. He did not quite mean to let go, but he did it, and immediately he was borne across the room.

'I flewed!' he screamed while still in mid-air.

John let go and met Wendy near the bathroom.

'Oh, lovely!'

'Oh, ripping!'

'Look at me!'

'Look at me!'

'Look at me!'

They were not nearly so elegant as Peter, they could not help kicking a little, but their heads were bobbing against the ceiling, and there is almost nothing so delicious as that. Peter gave Wendy a hand at first, but had to desist, Tink was so indignant.

Up and down they went, and round and round. Heavenly was Wendy's word.

'I say,' cried John, 'why shouldn't we all go out!'

Of course it was to this that Peter had been luring them.

Michael was ready: he wanted to see how long it took him to do a billion miles. But Wendy hesitated.

'Mermaids!' said Peter again.

'Oo!'

'And there are pirates.'

'Pirates,' cried John, seizing his Sunday hat, 'let us go at once.'

It was just at this moment that Mr and Mrs Darling hurried with Nana out of 27. They ran into the middle of the street to look up at the nursery window; and, yes, it was still shut, but the room was ablaze with light, and most heart-gripping sight of all, they could see in shadow on the curtain three little figures in night attire circling round and round, not on the floor but in the air.

Not three figures, four!

In a tremble they opened the street door. Mr Darling would have rushed upstairs, but Mrs Darling signed to him to go softly. She even tried to make her heart go softly.

Will they reach the nursery in time? If so, how delightful for them, and we shall all breathe a sigh of relief,

but there will be no story. On the other hand, if they are
not in time, I solemnly promise that it will all come right
in the end.

They would have reached the nursery in time had it
not been that the little stars were watching them. Once
again the stars blew the window open, and that smallest
star of all called out:

'Cave, Peter!'

Then Peter knew that there was not a moment to lose.
'Come,' he cried imperiously, and soared out at once
into the night followed by John and Michael and Wendy.

Mr and Mrs Darling and Nana rushed into the nursery
too late. The birds were flown.

4 The Flight

'Second to the right, and straight on till morning.'

That, Peter had told Wendy, was the way to the Neverland; but even birds, carrying maps and consulting them at windy corners, could not have sighted it with these instructions. Peter, you see, just said anything that came into his head.

At first his companions trusted him implicitly, and so great were the delights of flying that they wasted time circling round church spires or any other tall objects on the way that took their fancy.

John and Michael raced, Michael getting a start.

They recalled with contempt that not so long ago they had thought themselves fine fellows for being able to fly round a room.

Not so long ago. But how long ago? They were flying over the sea before this thought began to disturb Wendy seriously. John thought it was their second sea and their third night.

Sometimes it was dark and sometimes light, and now they were very cold and again too warm. Did they really feel hungry at times, or were they merely pretending because Peter had such a jolly new way of feeding them? His way was to pursue birds who had food in their mouths suitable for humans and snatch it from them; then the birds would follow and snatch it back; and they would all go chasing each other gaily for miles, parting at last with mutual expressions of good-will. But Wendy noticed with gentle concern that Peter did not seem to know that this was rather an odd way of getting your bread and butter, nor even that there are other ways.

Certainly they did not pretend to be sleepy, they were sleepy; and that was a danger, for the moment they popped off, down they fell. The awful thing was that Peter thought this funny.

'There he goes again!' he would cry gleefully, as Michael suddenly dropped like a stone.

'Save him, save him!' cried Wendy, looking with horror at the cruel sea far below. Eventually Peter would dive through the air, and catch Michael just before he could strike the sea, and it was lovely the way he did it; but he always waited till the last moment, and you felt it was his cleverness that interested him and not the saving of human life. Also he was fond of variety, and the sport that engrossed him one moment would suddenly cease to engage him, so there was always the possibility that the next time you fell he would let you go.

He could sleep in the air without falling, by merely lying on his back and floating, but this was, partly at least, because he was so light that if you got behind him and blew he went faster.

'Do be more polite to him,' Wendy whispered to John, when they were playing 'Follow my Leader'.

'Then tell him to stop showing off,' said John.

When playing Follow my Leader, Peter would fly close to the water and touch each shark's tail in passing, just as in the street you may run your finger along an iron railing. They could not follow him in this with much success, so perhaps it was rather like showing off, especially as he kept looking behind to see how many tails they missed.

'You must be nice to him,' Wendy impressed on her brothers. 'What would we do if he were to leave us?'

'We could go back,' Michael said.

'How could we ever find our way back without him?'

'Well, then, we could go on,' said John.

'That is the awful thing, John. We should have to go on, for we don't know how to stop.'

This was true; Peter had forgotten to show them how to stop.

John said that if the worst came to the worst, all they had to do was to go straight on, for the world was round, and so in time they must come back to their own window.

'And who is to get food for us, John?'

'I nipped a bit out of that eagle's mouth pretty neatly, Wendy.'

'After the twentieth try,' Wendy reminded him. 'And even though we became good at picking up food, see how we bump against clouds and things if he is not near to give us a hand.'

Indeed they were constantly bumping. They could now fly strongly, though they still kicked far too much; but if they saw a cloud in front of them, the more they tried to avoid it, the more certainly did they bump into it. If Nana had been with them she would have had a bandage round Michael's forehead by this time.

Peter was not with them for the moment, and they felt rather lonely up there by themselves. He could go so much faster than they that he would suddenly shoot out of sight, to have some adventure in which they had no share. He would come down laughing over something fearfully funny he had been saying to a star, but he had already forgotten what it was, or he would come up with mermaid scales still sticking to him, and yet not be able to say for certain what had been happening. It was really rather irritating to children who had never seen a mermaid.

'And if he forgets them so quickly,' Wendy argued, 'how can we expect that he will go on remembering us?'

Indeed, sometimes when he returned he did not remem-

ber them, at least not well. Wendy was sure of it. She
saw recognition come into his eyes as he was about to
pass them the time of day and go on; once even she had
to tell him her name.

'I'm Wendy,' she said agitatedly.

He was very sorry. 'I say, Wendy,' he whispered to

her, 'always if you see me forgetting you, just keep on saying "I'm Wendy", and then I'll remember.'

Of course this was rather unsatisfactory. However, to make amends he showed them how to lie out flat on a strong wind that was going their way, and this was such a pleasant change that they tried it several times and found they could sleep thus with security. Indeed they would have slept longer, but Peter tired quickly of sleeping, and soon he would cry in his captain voice, 'We get off here.' So with occasional tiffs, but on the whole rollicking, they drew near the Neverland; for after many moons they did reach it, and, what is more, they had been going pretty straight all the time, not perhaps so much owing to the guidance of Peter or Tink as because the island was out looking for them. It is only thus that anyone may sight those magic shores.

'There it is,' said Peter calmly.

'Where, where?'

'Where all the arrows are pointing.'

Indeed a million golden arrows were pointing out the island to the children, all directed by their friend the sun, who wanted them to be sure of their way before leaving them for the night.

Wendy and John and Michael stood on tiptoe in the air to get their first sight of the island. Strange to say, they all recognized it at once, and until fear fell upon them they hailed it, not as something long dreamt of and seen at last, but as a familiar friend to whom they were returning home for the holidays.

'John, there's the lagoon.'

'Wendy, look at the turtles burying their eggs in the sand.'

'I say, John, I see your flamingo with the broken leg.'

'Look, Michael, there's your cave.'

'John, what's that in the brushwood?'

'It's a wolf with her whelps. Wendy, I do believe that's your little whelp.'

'There's my boat, John, with her sides stove in.'

'No, it isn't. Why, we burned your boat.'

'That's her, at any rate. I say, John, I see the smoke of the redskin camp.'

'Where? Show me, and I'll tell you by the way the smoke curls whether they are on the war-path.'

'There, just across the Mysterious River.'

'I see now. Yes, they are on the war-path right enough.'

Peter was a little annoyed with them for knowing so much; but if he wanted to lord it over them his triumph was at hand, for have I not told you that anon fear fell upon them?

It came as the arrows went, leaving the island in gloom.

In the old days at home the Neverland had always begun to look a little dark and threatening by bedtime. Then unexplored patches arose in it and spread; black shadows moved about in them; the roar of the beasts of prey was quite different now, and above all, you lost the certainty that you would win. You were quite glad that the night-lights were on. You even liked Nana to say that this was just the mantelpiece over here, and that the Neverland was all make-believe.

Of course the Neverland had been make-believe in those days; but it was real now, and there were no night-lights, and it was getting darker every moment, and where was Nana?

They had been flying apart, but they huddled close to Peter now. His careless manner had gone at last, his eyes were sparkling, a tingle went through them every time they touched his body. They were now over the fearsome island, flying so low that sometimes a tree grazed their face. Nothing horrid was visible in the air, yet their progress had become slow and laboured, exactly as if they were pushing their way through hostile forces. Sometimes they hung in the air until Peter had beaten on it with his fists.

'They don't want us to land,' he explained.

'Who are they?' Wendy whispered, shuddering.

But he could not or would not say. Tinker Bell had been asleep on his shoulder, but now he wakened her and sent her on in front.

Sometimes he poised himself in the air, listening intently with his hand to his ear, and again he would stare down with eyes so bright that they seemed to bore two holes to earth. Having done these things, he went on again.

His courage was almost appalling. 'Do you want an adventure now,' he said casually to John, 'or would you like to have your tea first?'

Wendy said 'tea first' quickly, and Michael pressed her hand in gratitude, but the braver John hesitated.

'What kind of adventure?' he asked cautiously.

'There's a pirate asleep in the pampas just beneath us,' Peter told him. 'If you like, we'll go down and kill him.'

'I don't see him,' John said after a long pause.

'I do.'

'Suppose,' John said a little huskily, 'he were to wake up.'

Peter spoke indignantly. 'You don't think I would kill him while he was sleeping! I would wake him first, and then kill him. That's the way I always do.'

'I say! Do you kill many?'

'Tons.'

John said 'how ripping', but decided to have tea first. He asked if there were many pirates on the island just now, and Peter said he had never known so many.

'Who is captain now?'

'Hook,' answered Peter; and his face became very stern as he said that hated word.

'Jas. Hook?'

'Aye.'

Then indeed Michael began to cry, and even John could speak in gulps only, for they knew Hook's reputation.

'He was Blackbeard's bo'sun,' John whispered huskily. 'He is the worst of them all. He is the only man of whom Barbecue was afraid.'

'That's him,' said Peter.

'What is he like? Is he big?'

'He is not so big as he was.'

'How do you mean?'

'I cut off a bit of him.'

'You!'

'Yes, me,' said Peter sharply.

'I wasn't meaning to be disrespectful.'

'Oh, all right.'

'But, I say, what bit?'

'His right hand.'

'Then he can't fight now?'

'Oh, can't he just!'

'Left-hander?'

'He has an iron hook instead of a right hand, and he claws with it.'

'Claws!'

'I say, John,' said Peter.

'Yes.'

'Say, "Aye, aye, sir."'

'Aye, aye, sir.'

'There is one thing,' Peter continued, 'that every boy who serves under me had to promise, and so must you.'

John paled.

'It is this, if we meet Hook in open fight, you must leave him to me.'

'I promise,' John said loyally.

For the moment they were feeling less eerie, because Tink was flying with them, and in her light they could distinguish each other. Unfortunately she could not fly so slowly as they, and so she had to go round and round them in a circle in which they moved as in a halo. Wendy quite liked it, until Peter pointed out the drawback.

'She tells me,' he said, 'that the pirates sighted us before the darkness came, and got Long Tom out.'

'The big gun?'

'Yes. And of course they must see her light, and if they guess we are near it they are sure to let fly.'

'Wendy!'

'John!'

'Michael!'

'Tell her to go away at once, Peter,' the three cried simultaneously, but he refused.

'She thinks we have lost the way,' he replied stiffly, 'and she is rather frightened. You don't think I would send her away all by herself when she is frightened!'

For a moment the circle of light was broken, and something gave Peter a loving little pinch.

'Then tell her,' Wendy begged, 'to put out her light.'

'She can't put it out. That is about the only thing fairies can't do. It just goes out of itself when she falls asleep, same as the stars.'

'Then tell her to sleep at once,' John almost ordered.

'She can't sleep except when she's sleepy. It is the only other thing fairies can't do.'

'Seems to me,' growled John, 'these are the only two things worth doing.'

Here he got a pinch, but not a loving one.

'If only one of us had a pocket,' Peter said, 'we could carry her in it.' However, they had set off in such a hurry that there was not a pocket between the four of them.

He had a happy idea. John's hat!

Tink agreed to travel by hat if it was carried in the hand. John carried it, though she had hoped to be carried by Peter. Presently Wendy took the hat, because John said it struck against his knee as he flew; and this, as we shall see, led to mischief, for Tinker Bell hated to be under an obligation to Wendy.

In the black topper the light was completely hidden, and they flew on in silence. It was the stillest silence they had ever known, broken once by a distant lapping, which Peter explained was the wild beasts drinking at the ford, and again by a rasping sound that might have been the branches of trees rubbing together, but he said it was the redskins sharpening their knives.

Even these noises ceased. To Michael the loneliness was dreadful. 'If only something would make a sound!' he cried.

As if in answer to his request, the air was rent by the most tremendous crash he had ever heard. The pirates had fired Long Tom at them.

The roar of it echoed through the mountains, and the echoes seemed to cry savagely, 'Where are they, where are they, where are they?'

Thus sharply did the terrified three learn the difference between an island of make-believe and the same island come true.

When at last the heavens were steady again, John and Michael found themselves alone in the darkness. John was treading the air mechanically, and Michael without knowing how to float was floating.

'Are you shot?' John whispered tremulously.

'I haven't tried yet,' Michael whispered back.

We know now that no one had been hit. Peter, however, had been carried by the wind of the shot far out to sea, while Wendy was blown upwards with no companion but Tinker Bell.

It would have been well for Wendy if at that moment she had dropped the hat.

I don't know whether the idea came suddenly to Tink, or whether she had planned it on the way, but she at once popped out of the hat and began to lure Wendy to her destruction.

Tink was not all bad: or, rather, she was all bad just now, but, on the other hand, sometimes she was all good. Fairies have to be one thing or the other, because being so small they unfortunately have room for one feeling only at a time. They are, however, allowed to change, only it must be a complete change. At present she was full of jealousy of Wendy. What she said in her lovely tinkle Wendy could not of course understand, and I believe some of it was bad words, but it sounded kind, and she flew back and forward, plainly meaning 'Follow me, and all will be well.'

What else could poor Wendy do? She called to Peter and John and Michael, and got only mocking echoes in reply. She did not yet know that Tink hated her with the fierce hatred of a very woman. And so, bewildered, and now staggering in her flight, she followed Tink to her doom.

5 The Island Come True

Feeling that Peter was on his way back, the Neverland had again woke into life. We ought to use the pluperfect and say wakened, but woke is better and was always used by Peter.

In his absence things are usually quiet on the island. The fairies take an hour longer in the morning, the beasts attend to their young, the redskins feed heavily for six days and nights, and when pirates and lost boys meet they merely bite their thumbs at each other. But with the coming of Peter, who hates lethargy, they are all under way again: if you put your ear to the ground now, you would hear the whole island seething with life.

On this evening the chief forces of the island were disposed as follows. The lost boys were out looking for

Peter, the pirates were out looking for the lost boys, the redskins were out looking for the pirates, and the beasts were out looking for the redskins. They were going round and round the island, but they did not meet because all were going at the same rate.

All wanted blood except the boys, who liked it as a rule, but tonight were out to greet their captain. The boys on the island vary, of course, in numbers, according as they get killed and so on; and when they seem to be growing up, which is against the rules, Peter thins them out; but at this time there were six of them, counting the Twins as two. Let us pretend to lie here among the sugar-cane and watch them as they steal by in single file, each with his hand on his dagger.

They are forbidden by Peter to look in the least like him, and they wear the skins of bears slain by themselves, in which they are so round and furry that when they fall they roll. They have therefore become very sure-footed.

The first to pass is Tootles, not the least brave but the most unfortunate of all that gallant band. He had been in fewer adventures than any of them, because the big things constantly happened just when he had stepped round the corner; all would be quiet, he would take the opportunity of going off to gather a few sticks for firewood, and then when he returned the others would be sweeping up the blood. The ill luck had given a gentle melancholy to his countenance, but instead of souring his nature had sweetened it, so that he was quite the humblest of the boys. Poor kind Tootles, there is danger in the air for you tonight. Take care lest an adventure is now offered you, which, if accepted, will plunge you in deepest woe. Tootles, the fairy Tink, who is bent on mischief this night, is looking for a tool, and she thinks you the most easily tricked of the boys. 'Ware Tinker Bell.

Would that he could hear us, but we are not really on the island, and he passes by, biting his knuckles.

Next comes Nibs, the gay and debonair, followed by Slightly, who cuts whistles out of the trees and dances ecstatically to his own tunes. Slightly is the most conceited of the boys. He thinks he remembers the days before he was lost, with their manners and customs, and this has given his nose an offensive tilt. Curly is fourth; he is a pickle, and so often has he had to deliver up his person when Peter said sternly, 'Stand forth the one who did this thing,' that now at the command he stands forth automatically whether he has done it or not. Last come the Twins, who cannot be described because we should be sure to be describing the wrong one. Peter never quite knew what twins were, and his band were not allowed to know anything he did not know, so these two were always vague about themselves, and did their best to give satisfaction by keeping close together in an apologetic sort of way.

The boys vanish in the gloom, and after a pause, but not a long pause, for things go briskly on the island, come the pirates on their track. We hear them before they are seen, and it is always the same dreadful song:

> 'Avast belay, yo ho, heave to,
>   A-pirating we go,
> And if we're parted by a shot
>   We're sure to meet below!'

A more villainous-looking lot never hung in a row on Execution dock. Here, a little in advance, ever and again with his head to the ground listening, his great arms bare, pieces of eight in his ears as ornaments, is the handsome Italian Cecco, who cut his name in letters of blood on the back of the governor of the prison at Gao. That gigantic black behind him has had many names since he dropped the one with which dusky mothers still terrify their children on the banks of the Guidjo-mo. Here is Bill Jukes, every inch of him tattooed, the same Bill Jukes who got six dozen on the *Walrus* from Flint before he would drop the bag of moidores; and Cookson, said to be Black Murphy's brother (but this was never proved); and Gentleman Starkey, once an usher in a public school and still dainty in his ways of killing; and Skylights (Morgan's Skylights); and the Irish bo'sun Smee, an oddly genial man who stabbed, so to speak, without offence, and was the only Nonconformist in Hook's crew; and Noodler, whose hands were fixed on backwards; and Robt. Mullins and Alf Mason and many another ruffian long known and feared on the Spanish Main.

In the midst of them, the blackest and largest jewel in that dark setting, reclined James Hook, or, as he wrote

himself, Jas. Hook, of whom it is said he was the only
man that the Sea-Cook feared. He lay at his ease in a
rough chariot drawn and propelled by his men, and instead of a right hand he had the iron hook with which
ever and anon he encouraged them to increase their pace.
As dogs this terrible man treated and addressed them, and
as dogs they obeyed him. In person he was cadaverous
and blackavized, and his hair was dressed in long curls,
which at a little distance looked like black candles, and
gave a singularly threatening expression to his handsome
countenance. His eyes were of the blue of the forget-me-
not, and of a profound melancholy, save when he was
plunging his hook into you, at which time two red spots
appeared in them and lit them up horribly. In manner,

something of the grand seigneur still clung to him, so
that he even ripped you up with an air, and I have been
told that he was a *raconteur* of repute. He was never more
sinister than when he was most polite, which is probably
the truest test of breeding; and the elegance of his dic-
tion, even when he was swearing, no less than the dis-
tinction of his demeanour, showed him one of a different
caste from his crew. A man of indomitable courage, it
was said of him that the only thing he shied at was the
sight of his own blood, which was thick and of an unusual
colour. In dress he somewhat aped the attire associated
with the name of Charles II, having heard it said in
some earlier period of his career that he bore a strange
resemblance to the ill-fated Stuarts; and in his mouth he

had a holder of his own contrivance which enabled him to smoke two cigars at once. But undoubtedly the grimmest part of him was his iron claw.

Let us now kill a pirate, to show Hook's method. Skylights will do. As they pass, Skylights lurches clumsily against him, ruffling his lace collar; the hook shoots forth, there is a tearing sound and one screech, then the body is kicked aside, and the pirates pass on. He has not even taken the cigars from his mouth.

Such is the terrible man against whom Peter Pan is pitted. Which will win?

On the trail of the pirates, stealing noiselessly down the war-path, which is not visible to inexperienced eyes, come the redskins, every one of them with his eyes peeled. They carry tomahawks and knives, and their naked bodies gleam with paint and oil. Strung around them are scalps, of boys as well as of pirates, for these are the Piccaninny tribe, and not to be confused with the softer-hearted Delawares or the Hurons. In the van, on all fours, is Great Big Little Panther, a brave of so many scalps that in his present position they somewhat impede his progress. Bringing up the rear, the place of greatest danger, comes Tiger Lily, proudly erect, a princess in her own right. She is the most beautiful of dusky Dianas and the belle of the Piccaninnies, coquettish, cold and amorous by turns; there is not a brave who would not have the wayward thing to wife, but she staves off the altar with a hatchet. Observe how they pass over fallen twigs without making the slightest noise. The only sound to be heard is their somewhat heavy breathing. The fact is that they are all a little fat just now after the heavy gorging, but in time they will work this off. For the moment, however, it constitutes their chief danger.

The redskins disappear as they have come, like shadows, and soon their place is taken by the beasts, a great and motley procession: lions, tigers, bears, and the innumerable smaller savage things that flee from them, for every kind of beast, and, more particularly, all the man-eaters, live cheek by jowl on the favoured island. Their tongues are hanging out, they are hungry tonight.

When they have passed, comes the last figure of all, a gigantic crocodile. We shall see for whom she is looking presently.

The crocodile passes, but soon the boys appear again, for the procession must continue indefinitely until one of the parties stops or changes its pace. Then quickly they will be on top of each other.

All are keeping a sharp look out in front, but none suspects that the danger may be creeping up from behind. This shows how real the island was.

The first to fall out of the moving circle was the boys. They flung themselves down on the sward, close to their underground home.

'I do wish Peter would come back,' every one of them said nervously, though in height and still more in breadth they were all larger than their captain.

'I am the only one who is not afraid of the pirates,' Slightly said in the tone that prevented his being a general favourite; but perhaps some distant sound disturbed him, for he added hastily, 'but I wish he would come back, and tell us whether he has heard anything more about Cinderella.'

They talked of Cinderella, and Tootles was confident that his mother must have been very like her.

It was only in Peter's absence that they could speak of mothers, the subject being forbidden by him as silly.

'All I remember about my mother,' Nibs told them, 'is that she often said to father, "Oh, how I wish I had a cheque-book of my own." I don't know what a cheque-book is, but I should just love to give my mother one.'

While they talked they heard a distant sound. You or I, not being wild things of the woods, would have heard nothing, but they heard it, and it was the grim song:

'Yo ho, yo ho, the pirate life,
    The flag o' skull and bones,
A merry hour, a hempen rope,
    And hey for Davy Jones.'

At once the lost boys – but where are they? They are no longer there. Rabbits could not have disappeared more quickly.

I will tell you where they are. With the exception of Nibs, who has darted away to reconnoitre, they are already in their home under the ground, a very delightful residence of which we shall see a good deal presently. But how have they reached it? for there is no entrance to be seen, not so much as a pile of brushwood which, if removed, would disclose the mouth of a cave. Look closely, however, and you may note that there are here seven large trees, each having in its hollow trunk a hole as large as a boy. These are the seven entrances to the home under the ground, for which Hook has been searching in vain these many moons. Will he find it tonight?

As the pirates advanced, the quick eye of Starkey sighted Nibs disappearing through the wood, and at once his pistol flashed out. But an iron claw gripped his shoulder.

'Captain, let go,' he cried, writhing.

Now for the first time we hear the voice of Hook. It was a black voice. 'Put back that pistol first,' it said threateningly.

'It was one of those boys you hate. I could have shot him dead.'

'Aye, and the sound would have brought Tiger Lily's redskins upon us. Do you want to lose your scalp?'

'Shall I after him, captain,' asked pathetic Smee, 'and tickle him with Johnny Corkscrew?' Smee had pleasant names for everything, and his cutlass was Johnny Corkscrew, because he wriggled it in the wound. One could mention many lovable traits in Smee. For instance, after killing, it was his spectacles he wiped instead of his weapon.

'Johnny's a silent fellow,' he reminded Hook.

'Not now, Smee,' Hook said darkly. 'He is only one, and I want to mischief all the seven. Scatter and look for them.'

The pirates disappeared among the trees, and in a moment their captain and Smee were alone. Hook heaved a heavy sigh; and I know not why it was, perhaps it was because of the soft beauty of the evening, but there came over him a desire to confide to his faithful bo'sun the story of his life. He spoke long and earnestly, but what it was all about Smee, who was rather stupid, did not know in the least.

Anon he caught the word Peter.

'Most of all,' Hook was saying passionately, 'I want their captain, Peter Pan. 'Twas he cut off my arm.' He brandished the hook threateningly. 'I've waited long to shake his hand with this. Oh, I'll tear him.'

'And yet,' said Smee, 'I have often heard you say that hook was worth a score of hands, for combing the hair and other homely uses.'

'Aye,' the captain answered, 'if I was a mother I would pray to have my children born with this instead of that,' and he cast a look of pride upon his iron hand and one of scorn upon the other. Then again he frowned.

'Peter flung my arm,' he said, wincing, 'to a crocodile that happened to be passing by.'

'I have often,' said Smee, 'noticed your strange dread of crocodiles.'

'Not of crocodiles,' Hook corrected him, 'but of that one crocodile.' He lowered his voice. 'It liked my arm so much, Smee, that it has followed me ever since, from sea to sea and from land to land, licking its lips for the rest of me.'

'In a way,' said Smee, 'it's a sort of compliment.'

'I want no such compliments,' Hook barked petulantly. 'I want Peter Pan, who first gave the brute its taste for me.'

He sat down on a large mushroom, and now there was a quiver in his voice. 'Smee,' he said huskily, 'that crocodile would have had me before this, but by a lucky chance it swallowed a clock which goes tick tick inside it, and so before it can reach me I hear the tick and bolt.' He laughed, but in a hollow way.

'Some day,' said Smee, 'the clock will run down, and then he'll get you.'

Hook wetted his dry lips. 'Aye,' he said, 'that's the fear that haunts me.'

Since sitting down he had felt curiously warm. 'Smee,' he said, 'this seat is hot.' He jumped up. 'Odds bobs, hammer and tongs, I'm burning'

They examined the mushroom, which was of a size and solidity unknown on the mainland; they tried to pull it up, and it came away at once in their hands, for it had no root. Stranger still, smoke began at once to ascend. The pirates looked at each other. 'A chimney!' they both exclaimed.

They had indeed discovered the chimney of the home under the ground. It was the custom of the boys to stop it with a mushroom when enemies were in the neighbour-hood.

Not only smoke came out of it. There came also children's voices, for so safe did the boys feel in their hiding-place that they were gaily chattering. The pirates listened grimly, and then replaced the mushroom. They looked around them and noted the holes in the seven trees.

'Did you hear them say Peter Pan's from home?' Smee whispered, fidgeting with Johnny Corkscrew.

Hook nodded. He stood for a long time lost in thought, and at last a curdling smile lit up his swarthy face. Smee had been waiting for it. 'Unrip your plan, captain,' he cried eagerly.

'To return to the ship,' Hook replied slowly through his teeth, 'and cook a large rich cake of a jolly thickness with green sugar on it. There can be but one room below, for there is but one chimney. The silly moles had not the sense to see that they did not need a door apiece. That shows they have no mother. We will leave the cake on the shore of the mermaids' lagoon. These boys are always swimming about there, playing with the mermaids. They will find the cake and they will gobble it up, because, having no mother, they don't know how dangerous 'tis to eat rich damp cake.' He burst into laughter, not hollow laughter now, but honest laughter. 'Aha, they will die.'

Smee had listened with growing admiration.

'It's the wickedest, prettiest policy ever I heard of,' he cried, and in their exultation they danced and sang:

> 'Avast, belay, when I appear,
>   By fear they're overtook;
>   Naught's left upon your bones when you
>   Have shaken claws with Hook.'

They began the verse, but they never finished it, for another sound broke in and stilled them. It was at first

such a tiny sound that a leaf might have fallen on it and smothered it, but as it came nearer it was more distinct.

Tick tick tick tick.

Hook stood shuddering, one foot in the air.

'The crocodile,' he gasped, and bounded away, followed by his bo'sun.

It was indeed the crocodile. It had passed the redskins, who were now on the trail of the other pirates. It oozed on after Hook.

Once more the boys emerged into the open; but the dangers of the night were not yet over, for presently Nibs rushed breathless into their midst, pursued by a pack of wolves. The tongues of the pursuers were hanging out; the baying of them was horrible.

'Save me, save me!' cried Nibs, falling on the ground.

'But what can we do, what can we do?'

It was a high compliment to Peter that at that dire moment their thoughts turned to him.

'What would Peter do?' they cried simultaneously.

Almost in the same breath they added, 'Peter would look at them through his legs.'

And then, 'Let us do what Peter would do.'

It is quite the most successful way of defying wolves, and as one boy they bent and looked through their legs. The next moment is the long one; but victory came quickly, for as the boys advanced upon them in this terrible attitude, the wolves dropped their tails and fled.

Now Nibs rose from the ground, and the others thought that his staring eyes still saw the wolves. But it was not wolves he saw.

'I have seen a wonderfuller thing,' he cried as they gathered round him eagerly. 'A great white bird. It is flying this way.'

'What kind of a bird, do you think?'

'I don't know,' Nibs said, awestruck, 'but it looks so weary, and as it flies it moans, "Poor Wendy".'

'Poor Wendy?'

'I remember,' said Slightly instantly, 'there are birds called Wendies.'

'See, it comes,' cried Curly, pointing to Wendy in the heavens.

Wendy was now almost overhead, and they could hear her plaintive cry. But more distinct came the shrill voice of Tinker Bell. The jealous fairy had now cast off all disguise of friendship, and was darting at her victim from every direction, pinching savagely each time she touched.

'Hallo, Tink,' cried the wondering boys.

Tink's reply rang out: 'Peter wants you to shoot the Wendy.'

It was not in their nature to question when Peter ordered. 'Let us do what Peter wishes,' cried the simple boys. 'Quick, bows and arrows.'

All but Tootles popped down their trees. He had a bow and arrow with him, and Tink noted it, and rubbed her little hands.

'Quick, Tootles, quick,' she screamed. 'Peter will be so pleased.'

Tootles excitedly fitted the arrow to his bow. 'Out of the way, Tink,' he shouted; and then he fired, and Wendy fluttered to the ground with an arrow in her breast.

6 The Little House

Foolish Tootles was standing like a conqueror over Wendy's body when the other boys sprang, armed, from their trees.

'You are too late,' he cried proudly, 'I have shot the Wendy. Peter will be so pleased with me.'

Overhead Tinker Bell shouted 'Silly ass!' and darted into hiding. The others did not hear her. They had crowded round Wendy, and as they looked a terrible silence fell upon the wood. If Wendy's heart had been beating they would all have heard it.

Slightly was the first to speak. 'This is no bird,' he said in a scared voice. 'I think it must be a lady.'

'A lady?' said Tootles, and fell a-trembling.

'And we have killed her,' Nibs said hoarsely.

They all whipped off their caps.

'Now I see,' Curly said; 'Peter was bringing her to us.' He threw himself sorrowfully on the ground.

'A lady to take care of us at last,' said one of the twins, 'and you have killed her.'

They were sorry for him, but sorrier for themselves, and when he took a step nearer them they turned from him.

Tootles' face was very white, but there was a dignity about him now that had never been there before.

'I did it,' he said, reflecting. 'When ladies used to come to me in dreams, I said, "Pretty mother, pretty mother." But when at last she really came, I shot her.'

He moved slowly away.

'Don't go,' they called in pity.

'I must,' he answered, shaking; 'I am so afraid of Peter.'

It was at this tragic moment that they heard a sound which made the heart of every one of them rise to his mouth. They heard Peter crow.

'Peter!' they cried, for it was always thus that he signalled his return.

'Hide her,' they whispered, and gathered hastily around Wendy. But Tootles stood aloof.

Again came that ringing crow, and Peter dropped in front of them. 'Greeting, boys,' he cried, and mechanically they saluted, and then again was silence.

He frowned.

'I am back,' he said hotly, 'why do you not cheer?'

They opened their mouths, but the cheers would not come. He overlooked it in his haste to tell the glorious tidings.

'Great news, boys,' he cried. 'I have brought at last a mother for you all.'

Still no sound, except a little thud from Tootles as he dropped on his knees.

'Have you not seen her?' asked Peter, becoming troubled. 'She flew this way.'

'Ah me,' one voice said, and another said, 'Oh, mournful day.'

Tootles rose. 'Peter,' he said quietly, 'I will show her to you'; and when the others would still have hidden her he said, 'Back, twins, let Peter see.'

So they all stood back, and let him see, and after he had looked for a little time he did not know what to do next.

'She is dead,' he said uncomfortably. 'Perhaps she is frightened at being dead.'

He thought of hopping off in a comic sort of way till he was out of sight of her, and then never going near the spot any more. They would all have been glad to follow if he had done this.

But there was the arrow. He took it from her heart and faced his band.

'Whose arrow?' he demanded sternly.

'Mine, Peter,' said Tootles on his knees.

'Oh, dastard hand,' Peter said, and he raised the arrow to use it as a dagger.

Tootles did not flinch. He bared his breast. 'Strike, Peter,' he said firmly, 'strike true.'

Twice did Peter raise the arrow, and twice did his hand fall. 'I cannot strike,' he said with awe, 'there is something stays my hand.'

All looked at him in wonder, save Nibs, who fortunately looked at Wendy.

'It is she,' he cried, 'the Wendy lady; see, her arm.'

Wonderful to relate, Wendy had raised her arm. Nibs bent over her and listened reverently. 'I think she said "Poor Tootles",' he whispered.

'She lives,' Peter said briefly.

Slightly cried instantly, 'The Wendy lady lives.'

Then Peter knelt beside her and found his button. You remember she had put it on a chain that she wore round her neck.

'See,' he said, 'the arrow struck against this. It is the kiss I gave her. It has saved her life.'

'I remember kisses,' Slightly interposed quickly, 'let me see it. Aye, that's a kiss.'

Peter did not hear him. He was begging Wendy to get better quickly, so that he could show her the mermaids. Of course she could not answer yet, being still in a frightful faint; but from overhead came a wailing note.

'Listen to Tink,' said Curly, 'she is crying because the Wendy lives.'

Then they had to tell Peter of Tink's crime, and almost never had they seen him look so stern.

'Listen, Tinker Bell,' he cried; 'I am your friend no more. Begone from me for ever.'

She flew on to his shoulder and pleaded, but he brushed her off. Not until Wendy again raised her arm did he relent sufficiently to say, 'Well, not for ever, but for a whole week.'

Do you think Tinker Bell was grateful to Wendy for raising her arm? Oh dear no, never wanted to pinch her so much. Fairies indeed are strange, and Peter, who understood them best, often cuffed them.

But what to do with Wendy in her present delicate state of health?

'Let us carry her down into the house,' Curly suggested.

'Aye,' said Slightly, 'that is what one does with ladies.'

'No, no,' Peter said, 'you must not touch her. It would not be sufficiently respectful.'

'That,' said Slightly, 'is what I was thinking.'

'But if she lies there,' Tootles said, 'she will die.'

'Aye, she will die,' Slightly admitted, 'but there is no way out.'

'Yes, there is,' cried Peter. 'Let us build a little house round her.'

They were all delighted. 'Quick,' he ordered them, 'bring me each of you the best of what we have. Gut our house. Be sharp.'

In a moment they were as busy as tailors the night before a wedding. They skurried this way and that, down for bedding, up for firewood, and while they were at it, who should appear but John and Michael. As they dragged along the ground they fell asleep standing, stopped, woke up, moved another step and slept again.

'John, John,' Michael would cry, 'wake up. Where is Nana, John, and mother?'

And then John would rub his eyes and mutter, 'It is true, we did fly.'

You may be sure they were very relieved to find Peter.

'Hallo, Peter,' they said.

'Hallo,' replied Peter amicably, though he had quite forgotten them. He was very busy at the moment measuring Wendy with his feet to see how large a house she would need. Of course he meant to leave room for chairs and a table. John and Michael watched him.

'Is Wendy asleep?' they asked.

'Yes.'

'John,' Michael proposed, 'let us wake her and get her to make supper for us'; but as he said it some of the other boys rushed on carrying branches for the building of the house. 'Look at them!' he cried.

'Curly,' said Peter in his most captainy voice, 'see that these boys help in the building of the house.'

'Aye, aye, sir.'

'Build a house?' exclaimed John.

'For the Wendy,' said Curly.

'For Wendy?' John said aghast. 'Why, she is only a girl.'

'That,' explained Curly, 'is why we are her servants.'

'You? Wendy's servants!'

'Yes,' said Peter, 'and you also. Away with them.'

The astounded brothers were dragged away to hack and hew and carry. 'Chairs and a fender first,' Peter ordered. 'Then we shall build the house round them.'

'Aye,' said Slightly, 'that is how a house is built; it all comes back to me.'

Peter thought of everything. 'Slightly,' he ordered, 'fetch a doctor.'

'Aye, aye,' said Slightly at once, and disappeared, scratching his head. But he knew Peter must be obeyed, and he returned in a moment, wearing John's hat and looking solemn.

'Please, sir,' said Peter, going to him, 'are you a doctor?'

The difference between him and the other boys at such a time was that they knew it was make-believe, while to him make-believe and true were exactly the same thing. This sometimes troubled them, as when they had to make-believe that they had had their dinners.

If they broke down in their make-believe he rapped them on the knuckles.

'Yes, my little man,' anxiously replied Slightly, who had chapped knuckles.

'Please, sir,' Peter explained, 'a lady lies very ill.'

She was lying at their feet, but Slightly had the sense not to see her.

'Tut, tut, tut,' he said, 'where does she lie?'

'In yonder glade.'

'I will put a glass thing in her mouth,' said Slightly; and he made-believe to do it, while Peter waited. It was an anxious moment when the glass thing was withdrawn.

'How is she?' inquired Peter.

'Tut, tut, tut,' said Slightly, 'this has cured her.'

'I am glad,' Peter cried.

'I will call again in the evening,' Slightly said; 'give her beef tea out of a cup with a spout to it'; but after he had returned the hat to John he blew big breaths, which was his habit on escaping from a difficulty.

In the meantime the wood had been alive with the sound of axes; almost everything needed for a cosy dwelling already lay at Wendy's feet.

'If only we knew,' said one, 'the kind of house she likes best.'

'Peter,' shouted another, 'she is moving in her sleep.'

'Her mouth opens,' cried a third, looking respectfully into it. 'Oh, lovely!'

'Perhaps she is going to sing in her sleep,' said Peter. 'Wendy, sing the kind of house you would like to have.'

Immediately, without opening her eyes, Wendy began to sing:

> 'I wish I had a pretty house,
> The littlest ever seen,
> With funny little red walls
> And roof of mossy green.'

They gurgled with joy at this, for by the greatest good luck the branches they had brought were sticky with red sap, and all the ground was carpeted with moss. As they rattled up the little house they broke into song themselves:

'We've built the little walls and roof
    And made a lovely door,
So tell us, mother Wendy,
    What are you wanting more?'

To this she answered rather greedily:

'Oh, really, next I think I'll have
    Gay windows all about,
With roses peeping in, you know,
    And babies peeping out.'

With a blow of their fists they made windows, and large yellow leaves were the blinds. But roses – ?

'Roses,' cried Peter sternly.

Quickly they made-believe to grow the loveliest roses up the walls.

Babies?

To prevent Peter ordering babies they hurried into song again:

'We've made the roses peeping out,
    The babies are at the door,
We cannot make ourselves, you know,
    'Cos we've been made before.'

Peter, seeing this to be a good idea, at once pretended that it was his own. The house was quite beautiful, and no doubt Wendy was very cosy within, though, of course, they could no longer see her. Peter strode up and down, ordering finishing touches. Nothing escaped his eagle eye. Just when it seemed absolutely finished:

'There's no knocker on the door,' he said.

They were very ashamed, but Tootles gave the sole of his shoe, and it made an excellent knocker.

Absolutely finished now, they thought.

Not a bit of it. 'There's no chimney,' Peter said; 'we must have a chimney.'

'It certainly does need a chimney,' said John importantly. This gave Peter an idea. He snatched the hat off John's head, knocked out the bottom, and put the hat on the roof. The little house was so pleased to have such a capital chimney that, as if to say thank you, smoke immediately began to come out of the hat.

Now really and truly it was finished. Nothing remained to do but to knock.

'All look your best,' Peter warned them; 'first impressions are awfully important.'

He was glad no one asked him what first impressions are; they were all too busy looking their best.

He knocked politely; and now the wood was as still as the children, not a sound to be heard except from Tinker Bell, who was watching from a branch and openly sneering.

What the boys were wondering was, would anyone answer the knock? If a lady, what would she be like?

The door opened and a lady came out. It was Wendy. They all whipped off their hats.

She looked properly surprised, and this was just how they had hoped she would look.

'Where am I?' she said.

Of course Slightly was the first to get his word in. 'Wendy lady,' he said rapidly, 'for you we built this house.'

'Oh, say you're pleased,' cried Nibs.

'Lovely, darling house,' Wendy said, and they were the very words they had hoped she would say.

'And we are your children,' cried the twins.

Then all went on their knees, and holding out their arms cried, 'O Wendy lady, be our mother.'

'Ought I?' Wendy said, all shining. 'Of course it's frightfully fascinating, but you see I am only a little girl. I have no real experience.'

'That doesn't matter,' said Peter, as if he were the only person present who knew all about it, though he was really the one who knew least. 'What we need is just a nice motherly person.'

'Oh dear!' Wendy said, 'you see I feel that is exactly what I am.'

'It is, it is,' they all cried; 'we saw it at once.'

'Very well,' she said, 'I will do my best. Come inside at once, you naughty children; I am sure your feet are damp. And before I put you to bed I have just time to finish the story of Cinderella.'

In they went; I don't know how there was room for them, but you can squeeze very tight in the Neverland. And that was the first of the many joyous evenings they had with Wendy. By and by she tucked them up in the great bed in the home under the trees, but she herself slept that night in the little house, and Peter kept watch outside with drawn sword, for the pirates could be heard carousing far away and the wolves were on the prowl. The little house looked so cosy and safe in the darkness with a bright light showing through its blinds, and the chimney smoking beautifully, and Peter standing on guard.

After a time he fell asleep, and some unsteady fairies had to climb over him on their way home from an orgy. Any of the other boys obstructing the fairy path at night they would have mischiefed, but they just tweaked Peter's nose and passed on.

7 The Home Under the Ground

One of the first things Peter did next day was to measure Wendy and John and Michael for hollow trees. Hook, you remember, had sneered at the boys for thinking they needed a tree apiece, but this was ignorance, for unless your tree fitted you it was difficult to go up and down, and no two of the boys were quite the same size. Once you fitted, you drew in your breath at the top, and down you went at exactly the right speed, while to ascend you drew in and let out alternately, and so wriggled up. Of course, when you have mastered the action you are able to do these things without thinking of them, and then nothing can be more graceful.

But you simply must fit, and Peter measures you for your tree as carefully as for a suit of clothes: the only difference being that the clothes are made to fit you, while you have to be made to fit the tree. Usually it is done quite easily, as by your wearing too many garments or too few; but if you are bumpy in awkward places or the only available tree is an odd shape, Peter does some things to you, and after that you fit. Once you fit, great care must be taken to go on fitting, and this, as Wendy was to discover to her delight, keeps a whole family in perfect condition.

Wendy and Michael fitted their trees at the first try, but John had to be altered a little.

After a few days' practice they could go up and down as gaily as buckets in a well. And how ardently they grew to love their home under the ground; especially Wendy. It consisted of one large room, as all houses should do, with a floor in which you could dig if you wanted to go fish-

ing, and in this floor grew stout mushrooms of a charming colour, which were used as stools. A Never tree tried
hard to grow in the centre of the room, but every morning
they sawed the trunk through, level with the floor. By
tea-time it was always about two feet high, and then they
put a door on top of it, the whole thus becoming a table;
as soon as they cleared away, they sawed off the trunk
again, and thus there was more room to play. There was
an enormous fire-place which was in almost any part of
the room where you cared to light it, and across this
Wendy stretched strings, made of fibre, from which she
suspended her washing. The bed was tilted against the
wall by day, and let down at 6.30, when it filled nearly
half the room; and all the boys except Michael slept in
it, lying like sardines in a tin. There was a strict rule
against turning round until one gave the signal, when all
turned at once. Michael should have used it also; but
Wendy would have a baby, and he was the littlest, and
you know what women are, and the short and the long of
it is that he was hung up in a basket.

It was rough and simple, and not unlike what baby
bears would have made of an underground house in the
same circumstances. But there was one recess in the wall,
no larger than a bird-cage, which was the private apart-
ment of Tinker Bell. It could be shut off from the rest
of the home by a tiny curtain, which Tink, who was most
fastidious, always kept drawn when dressing or undress-
ing. No woman, however large, could have had a more
exquisite boudoir and bedchamber combined. The couch,
as she always called it, was a genuine Queen Mab, with
club legs; and she varied the bedspreads according to
what fruit-blossom was in season. Her mirror was a
Puss-in-boots, of which there are now only three, un-
chipped, known to the fairy dealers; the wash-stand was
Pie-crust and reversible, the chest of drawers an authentic

Charming the Sixth, and the carpet and rugs of the best (the early) period of Margery and Robin. There was a chandelier from Tiddlywinks for the look of the thing, but of course she lit the residence herself. Tink was very contemptuous of the rest of the house, as indeed was perhaps inevitable; and her chamber, though beautiful, looked rather conceited, having the appearance of a nose permanently turned up.

I suppose it was all especially entrancing to Wendy, because those rampagious boys of hers gave her so much to do. Really there were whole weeks when, except perhaps with a stocking in the evening, she was never above ground. The cooking, I can tell you, kept her nose to the pot. Their chief food was roasted bread-fruit, yams, coconuts, baked pig, mammee-apples, tappa rolls and bananas, washed down with calabashes of poe-poe; but you never exactly knew whether there would be a real meal or just a make-believe, it all depended upon Peter's whim. He could eat, really eat, if it was part of a game, but he could not stodge just to feel stodgy, which is what most children like better than anything else; the next best thing being to talk about it. Make-believe was so real to him that during a meal of it you could see him getting rounder. Of course it was trying, but you simply had to follow his lead, and if you could prove to him that you were getting loose for your tree he let you stodge.

Wendy's favourite time for sewing and darning was after they had all gone to bed. Then, as she expressed it, she had a breathing time for herself; and she occupied it in making new things for them, and putting double pieces on the knees, for they were all most frightfully hard on their knees.

When she sat down to a basketful of their stockings, every heel with a hole in it, she would fling up her arms and exclaim, 'Oh dear, I am sure I sometimes think spinsters are to be envied.'

Her face beamed when she exclaimed this.

You remember about her pet wolf. Well, it very soon discovered that she had come to the island and it found her out, and they just ran into each other's arms. After that it followed her about everywhere.

As time wore on did she think much about the beloved parents she had left behind her? This is a difficult question, because it is quite impossible to say how time does wear on in the Neverland, where it is calculated by moons and suns, and there are ever so many more of them than on the mainland. But I am afraid that Wendy did not really worry about her father and mother; she was absolutely confident that they would always keep the window open for her to fly back by, and this gave her complete ease of mind. What did disturb her at times was that John remembered his parents vaguely only, as people he had once known, while Michael was quite willing to believe that she was really his mother. These things scared her a little, and nobly anxious to do her duty, she tried to fix the old life in their minds by setting them examination papers on it, as like as possible to the ones she used to do at school. The other boys thought this awfully interesting and insisted on joining, and they made slates for themselves, and sat round the table, writing and thinking hard about the questions she had written on another slate and passed round. They were the most ordinary questions – 'What was the colour of Mother's eyes? Which was taller, Father or Mother? Was Mother blonde or brunette? Answer all three questions if possible.' '(A) Write an essay of not less than 40 words on How I spent my last Holidays, or The Characters of Father and Mother compared. Only one of these to be attempted.' Or '(1) Describe Mother's laugh; (2) Describe Father's laugh; (3) Describe Mother's Party Dress; (4) Describe the Kennel and its Inmate.'

They were just everyday questions like these, and when you could not answer them you were told to make a cross and it was really dreadful what a number of crosses even John made. Of course the only boy who replied to every question was Slightly, and no one could have been more hopeful of coming out first, but his answers were perfectly ridiculous, and he really came out last: a melancholy thing.

Peter did not compete. For one thing he despised all mothers except Wendy, and for another he was the only boy on the island who could neither write nor spell; not the smallest word. He was above all that sort of thing.

By the way, the questions were all written in the past tense. What was the colour of Mother's eyes, and so on. Wendy, you see, had been forgetting too.

Adventures, of course, as we shall see, were of daily occurrence; but about this time Peter invented, with Wendy's help, a new game that fascinated him enormously, until he suddenly had no more interest in it, which, as you have been told, was what always happened with his games. It consisted in pretending not to have adventures, in doing the sort of thing John and Michael had been doing all their lives: sitting on stools flinging balls in the air, pushing each other, going out for walks and coming back without having killed so much as a grizzly. To see Peter doing nothing on a stool was a great sight; he could not help looking solemn at such times, to sit still seemed to him such a comic thing to do. He boasted that he had gone a walk for the good of his health. For several suns these were the most novel of all adventures to him; and John and Michael had to pretend to be delighted also; otherwise he would have treated them severely.

He often went out alone, and when he came back you were never absolutely certain whether he had had an adventure or not. He might have forgotten it so completely that he said nothing about it; and then when you went out you found the body; and, on the other hand, he might say a great deal about it, and yet you could not find the body. Sometimes he came home with his head bandaged, and then Wendy cooed over him and bathed it in lukewarm water, while he told a dazzling tale. But she was never quite sure, you know. There were, however, many adventures which she knew to be true because she was in them herself, and there were still more that were at least partly true, for the other boys were in them and said they were wholly true. To describe them all would require a book as large as an English–Latin, Latin–English Dictionary, and the most we can do is to give one as a specimen of an average hour on the island. The difficulty is which one to choose. Should we take the brush with the redskins at Slightly Gulch? It was a sanguinary affair, and especially interesting as showing one of Peter's peculiarities, which was that in the middle of a fight he would suddenly change sides. At the Gulch, when victory was still in the balance, sometimes leaning this way and sometimes that, he called out, 'I'm redskin today; what are you, Tootles?' And Tootles answered, 'Redskin; what are you, Nibs?' and Nibs said, 'Redskin; what are you, Twin?' and so on; and they were all redskin; and of course this would have ended the fight had not the real redskins, fascinated by Peter's methods, agreed to be lost boys for that once, and so at it they all went again, more fiercely than ever.

The extraordinary upshot of this adventure was – but

we have not decided yet that this is the adventure we are to narrate. Perhaps a better one would be the night attack by the redskins on the house under the ground, when several of them stuck in the hollow trees and had to be pulled out like corks. Or we might tell how Peter saved Tiger Lily's life in the Mermaids' Lagoon, and so made her his ally.

Or we could tell of that cake the pirates cooked so that the boys might eat it and perish; and how they placed it in one cunning spot after another; but always Wendy snatched it from the hands of her children, so that in time it lost its succulence, and became as hard as a stone, and was used as a missile, and Hook fell over it in the dark.

Or suppose we tell of the birds that were Peter's friends, particularly of the Never bird that built in a tree overhanging the lagoon, and how the nest fell into the water, and still the bird sat on her eggs, and Peter gave orders that she was not to be disturbed. That is a pretty story, and the end shows how grateful a bird can be; but if we tell it we must also tell the whole adventure of the lagoon, which would of course be telling two adventures rather than just one. A shorter adventure, and quite as exciting, was Tinker Bell's attempt, with the help of some street fairies, to have the sleeping Wendy conveyed on a great floating leaf to the mainland. Fortunately the leaf gave way and Wendy woke, thinking it was bath-time, and swam back. Or again, we might choose Peter's defiance of the lions, when he drew a circle round him on the ground with an arrow and defied them to cross it; and though he waited for hours, with the other boys and Wendy looking on breathlessly from trees, not one of them dared to accept his challenge.

Which of these adventures shall we choose? The best way will be to toss for it.

I have tossed, and the lagoon has won. This almost makes one wish that the gulch or the cake or Tink's leaf had won. Of course I could do it again, and make it best out of three; however, perhaps fairest to stick to the lagoon.

8 The Mermaids' Lagoon

If you shut your eyes and are a lucky one, you may see at times a shapeless pool of lovely pale colours suspended in the darkness; then if you squeeze your eyes tighter, the pool begins to take shape, and the colours become so vivid that with another squeeze they must go on fire. But just before they go on fire you see the lagoon. This is the nearest you ever get to it on the mainland, just one heavenly moment; if there could be two moments you might see the surf and hear the mermaids singing.

The children often spent long summer days on this lagoon, swimming or floating most of the time, playing the mermaid games in the water and so forth. You must not think from this that the mermaids were on friendly terms with them; on the contrary, it was among Wendy's lasting regrets that all the time she was on the island she never had a civil word from one of them. When she stole softly to the edge of the lagoon she might see them by the score, especially on the Marooners' Rock, where they loved to bask, combing out their hair in a lazy way that quite irritated her; or she might even swim, on tiptoe as it were, to within a yard of them, but then they saw her and dived, probably splashing her with their tails, not by accident, but intentionally.

They treated all the boys in the same way, except of course Peter, who chatted with them on Marooners' Rock by the hour, and sat on their tails when they got cheeky. He gave Wendy one of their combs.

The most haunting time at which to see them is at the turn of the moon, when they utter strange wailing cries;

but the lagoon is dangerous for mortals then, and until the evening of which we have now to tell, Wendy had never seen the lagoon by moonlight, less from fear, for of course Peter would have accompanied her, than because she had strict rules about every one being in bed by seven. She was often at the lagoon, however, on sunny days after rain, when the mermaids come up in extraordinary numbers to play with their bubbles. The bubbles of many colours made in rainbow water they treat as balls, hitting them gaily from one to another with their tails, and trying to keep them in the rainbow till they burst. The goals are at each end of the rainbow, and the keepers only are allowed to use their hands. Sometimes hundreds of mermaids will be playing in the lagoon at a time, and it is quite a pretty sight.

But the moment the children tried to join in they had to play by themselves, for the mermaids immediately disappeared. Nevertheless we have proof that they secretly watched the interlopers, and were not above taking an idea from them; for John introduced a new way of hitting the bubble, with the head instead of the hand, and the mermaid goal-keepers adopted it. This is the one mark that John has left on the Neverland.

It must also have been rather pretty to see the children resting on a rock for half an hour after their midday meal. Wendy insisted on their doing this, and it had to be a real rest even though the meal was make-believe. So they lay there in the sun, and their bodies glistened in it, while she sat beside them and looked important.

It was one such day, and they were all on Marooners' Rock. The rock was not much larger than their great bed, but of course they all knew how not to take up much room, and they were dozing, or at least lying with their eyes shut, and pinching occasionally when they thought Wendy was not looking. She was very busy, stitching.

While she stitched a change came to the lagoon. Little shivers ran over it, and the sun went away and shadows stole across the water, turning it cold. Wendy could no longer see to thread her needle, and when she looked up, the lagoon that had always hitherto been such a laughing place seemed formidable and unfriendly.

It was not, she knew, that night had come, but something as dark as night had come. No, worse than that. It had not come, but it had sent that shiver through the sea to say that it was coming. What was it?

There crowded upon her all the stories she had been told of Marooners' Rock, so called because evil captains put sailors on it and leave them there to drown. They drown when the tide rises, for then it is submerged.

Of course she should have roused the children at once; not merely because of the unknown that was stalking towards them, but because it was no longer good for them to sleep on a rock grown chilly. But she was a young mother and she did not know this; she thought you simply must stick to your rule about half an hour after the midday meal. So, though fear was upon her, and she longed to hear male voices, she would not waken them. Even when she heard the sound of muffled oars, though her heart was in her mouth, she did not waken them. She stood over them to let them have their sleep out. Was it not brave of Wendy?

It was well for those boys then that there was one among them who could sniff danger even in his sleep. Peter sprang erect, as wide awake at once as a dog, and with one warning cry he roused the others.

He stood motionless, one hand to his ear.

'Pirates!' he cried. The others came closer to him. A strange smile was playing about his face, and Wendy saw it and shuddered. While that smile was on his face no one dared address him; all they could do was to stand ready to obey. The order came sharply and incisive.

'Dive!'

There was a gleam of legs, and instantly the lagoon seemed deserted. Marooners' Rock stood alone in the forbidding waters, as if it were itself marooned.

The boat drew nearer. It was the pirate dinghy, with three figures in her, Smee and Starkey, and the third a captive, no other than Tiger Lily. Her hands and ankles were tied, and she knew what was to be her fate. She was to be left on the rock to perish, an end to one of her race more terrible than death by fire or torture, for is it not written in the book of the tribe that there is no path through water to the happy hunting-ground? Yet her face was impassive; she was the daughter of a chief, she must die as a chief's daughter, it is enough.

They had caught her boarding the pirate ship with a knife in her mouth. No watch was kept on the ship, it being Hook's boast that the wind of his name guarded the

ship for a mile around. Now her fate would help to guard it also. One more wail would go the round in that wind by night.

In the gloom that they brought with them the two pirates did not see the rock till they crashed into it.

'Luff, you lubber,' cried an Irish voice that was Smee's; 'here's the rock. Now, then, what we have to do is to hoist the redskin on to it, and leave her there to drown.'

It was the work of one brutal moment to land the beautiful girl on the rock; she was too proud to offer a vain resistance.

Quite near the rock, but out of sight, two heads were bobbing up and down, Peter's and Wendy's. Wendy was crying, for it was the first tragedy she had seen. Peter had seen many tragedies, but he had forgotten them all. He was less sorry than Wendy for Tiger Lily; it was two againt one that angered him, and he meant to save her. An easy way would have been to wait until the pirates had gone, but he was never one to choose the easy way.

There was almost nothing he could not do, and he now imitated the voice of Hook.

'Ahoy there, you lubbers,' he called. It was a marvellous imitation.

'The captain,' said the pirates, staring at each other in surprise.

'He must be swimming out to us,' Starkey said, when they had looked for him in vain.

'We are putting the redskin on the rock,' Smee called out.

'Set her free,' came the astonishing answer.

'Free!'

'Yes, cut her bonds and let her go.'

'But, captain –'

'At once, d'ye hear,' cried Peter, 'or I'll plunge my hook in you.'

'This is queer,' Smee gasped.

'Better do what the captain orders,' said Starkey nervously.

'Aye, aye,' Smee said, and he cut Tiger Lily's cords. At once like an eel she slid between Starkey's legs into the water.

Of course Wendy was very elated over Peter's cleverness; but she knew that he would be elated also and very likely crow and thus betray himself, so at once her hand went out to cover his mouth. But it was stayed even in the act, for 'Boat ahoy!' rang over the lagoon in Hook's voice, and this time it was not Peter who had spoken.

Peter may have been about to crow, but his face puckered in a whistle of surprise instead.

'Boat ahoy!' again came the cry.

Now Wendy understood. The real Hook was also in the water.

He was swimming to the boat, and as his men showed a light to guide him he had soon reached them. In the light of the lantern Wendy saw his hook grip the boat's side; she saw his evil swarthy face as he rose dripping from the water, and, quaking, she would have liked to swim away, but Peter would not budge. He was tingling with life and also top-heavy with conceit. 'Am I not a wonder, oh, I am a wonder!' he whispered to her; and though she thought so also, she was really glad for the sake of his reputation that no one heard him except herself.

He signed to her to listen.

The two pirates were very curious to know what had brought their captain to them, but he sat with his head on his hook in a position of profound melancholy.

'Captain, is all well?' they asked timidly, but he answered with a hollow moan.

'He sighs,' said Smee.

'He sighs again,' said Starkey.

'And yet a third time he sighs,' said Smee.

'What's up, captain?'

Then at last he spoke passionately.

'The game's up,' he cried, 'those boys have found a mother.'

Affrighted though she was, Wendy swelled with pride.

'O evil day,' cried Starkey.

'What's a mother?' asked the ignorant Smee.

Wendy was so shocked that she exclaimed, 'He doesn't know!' and always after this she felt that if you could have a pet pirate Smee would be her one.

Peter pulled her beneath the water, for Hook had started up, crying, 'What was that?'

'I heard nothing,' said Starkey, raising the lantern over the waters, and as the pirates looked they saw a strange sight. It was the nest I have told you of, floating on the lagoon, and the Never bird was sitting on it.

'See,' said Hook in answer to Smee's question, 'that is a mother. What a lesson! The nest must have fallen into the water, but would the mother desert her eggs? No.'

There was a break in his voice, as if for a moment he recalled innocent days when – but he brushed away this weakness with his hook.

Smee, much impressed, gazed at the bird as the nest

was borne past, but the more suspicious Starkey said, 'If she is a mother, perhaps she is hanging about here to help Peter.'

Hook winced. 'Aye,' he said, 'that is the fear that haunts me.'

He was roused from this dejection by Smee's eager voice.

'Captain,' said Smee, 'could we not kidnap these boys' mother and make her our mother?'

'It is a princely scheme,' cried Hook, and at once it took practical shape in his great brain. 'We will seize the children and carry them to the boat: the boys we will make walk the plank, and Wendy shall be our mother.'

Again Wendy forgot herself.

'Never!' she cried, and bobbed.

'What was that?'

But they could see nothing. They thought it must have been but a leaf in the wind. 'Do you agree, my bullies?' asked Hook.

'There is my hand on it,' they both said.

'And there is my hook. Swear.'

They all swore. By this time they were on the rock and suddenly Hook remembered Tiger Lily.

'Where is the redskin?' he demanded abruptly.

He had a playful humour at moments, and they thought this was one of the moments.

'That is all right, captain,' Smee answered complacently, 'we let her go.'

'Let her go!' cried Hook.

' 'Twas your own orders,' the bos'un faltered.

'You called over the water to us to let her go,' said Starkey.

'Brimstone and gall,' thundered Hook, 'what cozening is here?' His face had gone black with rage, but he saw that they believed their words, and he was startled.

'Lads,' he said, shaking a little, 'I gave no such order.'

'It is passing queer,' Smee said, and they all fidgeted uncomfortably. Hook raised his voice, but there was a quiver in it.

'Spirit that haunts this dark lagoon tonight,' he cried, 'dost hear me?'

Of course Peter should have kept quiet, but of course he did not. He immediately answered in Hook's voice:

'Odds, bobs, hammer and tongs, I hear you.'

In that supreme moment Hook did not blanch, even at the gills, but Smee and Starkey clung to each other in terror.

'Who are you, stranger, speak?' Hook demanded.

'I am James Hook,' replied the voice, 'captain of the *Jolly Roger*.'

'You are not; you are not,' Hook cried hoarsely.

'Brimstone and gall,' the voice retorted, 'say that again, and I'll cast anchor in you.'

Hook tried a more ingratiating manner. 'If you are Hook,' he said almost humbly, 'come, tell me, who am I?'

'A codfish,' replied the voice, 'only a codfish.'

'A codfish!' Hook echoed blankly; and it was then, but not till then, that his proud spirit broke. He saw his men draw back from him.

'Have we been captained all this time by a codfish?' they muttered. 'It is lowering to our pride.'

They were his dogs snapping at him, but, tragic figure though he had become, he scarcely heeded them. Against such fearful evidence it was not their belief in him that he needed, it was his own. He felt his ego slipping from him. 'Don't desert me, bully,' he whispered hoarsely to it.

In the dark nature there was a touch of the feminine, as in all the great pirates, and it sometimes gave him intuitions. Suddenly he tried the guessing game.

'Hook,' he called, 'have you another voice?'

Now Peter could never resist a game, and he answered blithely in his own voice, 'I have.'

'And another name?'

'Aye, aye.'

'Vegetable?' asked Hook.

'No.'

'Mineral?'

'No.'

'Animal?'

'Yes.'

'Man?'

'No!' This answer rang out scornfully.

'Boy?'

'Yes.'

'Ordinary boy?'

'No!'

'Wonderful boy?'

To Wendy's pain the answer that rang out this time was 'Yes.'

'Are you in England?'

'No.'

'Are you here?'

'Yes.'

Hook was completely puzzled. 'You ask him some questions,' he said to the others, wiping his damp brow.

Smee reflected. 'I can't think of a thing,' he said regretfully.

'Can't guess, can't guess,' crowed Peter. 'Do you give it up?'

Of course in his pride he was carrying the game too far, and the miscreants saw their chance.

'Yes, yes,' they answered eagerly.

'Well, then,' he cried, 'I am Peter Pan.'

Pan!

In a moment Hook was himself again, and Smee and Starkey were his faithful henchmen.

'Now we have him,' Hook shouted. 'Into the water, Smee. Starkey, mind the boat. Take him dead or alive.'

He leaped as he spoke, and simultaneously came the gay voice of Peter.

'Are you ready, boys?'

'Aye, aye,' from various parts of the lagoon.

'Then lam into the pirates.'

The fight was short and sharp. First to draw blood was John, who gallantly climbed into the boat and held Starkey. There was a fierce struggle, in which the cutlass was torn from the pirate's grasp. He wriggled overboard and John leapt after him. The dinghy drifted away.

Here and there a head bobbed up in the water, and there was a flash of steel, followed by a cry or a whoop. In the confusion some struck at their own side. The corkscrew of Smee got Tootles in the fourth rib, but he was himself pinked in turn by Curly. Farther from the rock Starkey was pressing Slightly and the twins hard.

Where all this time was Peter? He was seeking bigger game.

The others were all brave boys, and they must not be blamed for backing from the pirate captain. His iron claw made a circle of dead water round him, from which they fled like affrighted fishes.

But there was one who did not fear him: there was one prepared to enter that circle.

Strangely, it was not in the water that they met. Hook rose to the rock to breathe, and at the same moment Peter scaled it on the opposite side. The rock was slippery as a ball, and they had to crawl rather than climb. Neither knew that the other was coming. Each feeling for a grip met the other's arm: in surprise they raised their heads; their faces were almost touching; so they met.

Some of the greatest heroes have confessed that just before they fell to they had a sinking. Had it been so with Peter at that moment I would admit it. After all, this was the only man that the Sea-Cook had feared. But Peter had no sinking, he had one feeling only, gladness; and he gnashed his pretty teeth with joy. Quick as thought he snatched a knife from Hook's belt and was about to drive it home, when he saw that he was higher up the rock than his foe. It would not have been fighting fair. He gave the pirate a hand to help him up.

It was then that Hook bit him.

Not the pain of this but its unfairness was what dazed

Peter. It made him quite helpless. He could only stare, horrified. Every child is affected thus the first time he is treated unfairly. All he thinks he has a right to when he comes to you to be yours is fairness. After you have been unfair to him he will love you again, but he will never afterwards be quite the same boy. No one ever gets over the first unfairness; no one except Peter. He often met it, but he always forgot it. I suppose that was the real difference between him and all the rest.

So when he met it now it was like the first time; and he could just stare, helpless. Twice the iron hand clawed him.

A few minutes afterwards the other boys saw Hook in the water striking wildly for the ship; no elation on his pestilent face now, only white fear, for the crocodile was in dogged pursuit of him. On ordinary occasions the boys would have swum alongside cheering; but now they were uneasy, for they had lost both Peter and Wendy, and were scouring the lagoon for them, calling them by name. They found the dinghy and went home in it, shouting, 'Peter, Wendy,' as they went, but no answer came save mocking laughter from the mermaids. 'They must be swimming back or flying,' the boys concluded. They were not very anxious, they had such faith in Peter. They chuckled, boylike, because they would be late for bed; and it was all Mother Wendy's fault!

When their voices died away there came cold silence over the lagoon, and then a feeble cry.

'Help, help!'

Two small figures were beating against the rock; the girl had fainted and lay on the boy's arm. With a last effort Peter pulled her up the rock and then lay down beside her. Even as he also fainted he saw that the water was rising. He knew that they would soon be drowned, but he could do no more.

As they lay side by side a mermaid caught Wendy by the feet, and began pulling her softly into the water. Peter, feeling her slip from him, woke with a start, and was just in time to draw her back. But he had to tell her the truth.

'We are on the rock, Wendy,' he said, 'but it is growing smaller. Soon the water will be over it.'

She did not understand even now.

'We must go,' she said almost brightly.

'Yes,' he answered faintly.

'Shall we swim or fly, Peter?'

He had to tell her.

'Do you think you could swim or fly as far as the island, Wendy, without my help?'

She had to admit that she was too tired.

He moaned.

'What is it?' she asked, anxious about him at once.

'I can't help you, Wendy. Hook wounded me. I can neither fly nor swim.'

'Do you mean we shall both be drowned?'

'Look how the water is rising.'

They put their hands over their eyes to shut out the sight. They thought they would soon be no more. As they sat thus something brushed against Peter as light as a kiss, and stayed there, as if saying timidly, 'Can I be of any use?'

It was the tail of a kite, which Michael had made some days before. It had torn itself out of his hand and floated away.

'Michael's kite,' Peter said without interest, but next moment he had seized the tail, and was pulling the kite towards him.

'It lifted Michael off the ground,' he cried; 'why should it not carry you?'

'Both of us!'

'It can't lift two; Michael and Curly tried.'

'Let us draw lots,' Wendy said bravely.

'And you a lady; never.' Already he had tied the tail round her. She clung to him; she refused to go without him; but with a 'Good-bye, Wendy,' he pushed her from the rock; and in a few minutes she was borne out of his sight. Peter was alone on the lagoon.

The rock was very small now; soon it would be submerged. Pale rays of light tiptoed across the waters; and by and by there was to be heard a sound at once the most musical and the most melancholy in the world; the mermaids calling to the moon.

Peter was not quite like other boys; but he was afraid at last. A tremor ran through him, like a shudder passing over the sea; but on the sea one shudder follows another till there are hundreds of them, and Peter felt just the one. Next moment he was standing erect on the rock again, with that smile on his face and a drum beating within him. It was saying, 'To die will be an awfully big adventure.'

9 The Never Bird

The last sounds Peter heard before he was quite alone were the mermaids retiring one by one to their bedchambers under the sea. He was too far away to hear their doors shut; but every door in the coral caves where they live rings a tiny bell when it opens or closes (as in all the nicest houses on the mainland), and he heard the bells.

Steadily the waters rose till they were nibbling at his feet; and to pass the time until they made their final gulp, he watched the only thing moving on the lagoon. He thought it was a piece of floating paper, perhaps part of the kite, and wondered idly how long it would take to drift ashore.

Presently he noticed as an odd thing that it was undoubtedly out upon the lagoon with some definite purpose, for it was fighting the tide, and sometimes winning; and when it won, Peter, always sympathetic to the weaker side, could not help clapping; it was such a gallant piece of paper.

It was not really a piece of paper; it was the Never bird, making desperate efforts to reach Peter on her nest. By working her wings, in a way she had learned since the nest fell into the water, she was able to some extent to guide her strange craft, but by the time Peter recognized her she was very exhausted. She had come to save him, to give him her nest, though there were eggs in it. I rather wonder at the bird, for though he had been nice to her, he had also sometimes tormented her. I can suppose only that, like Mrs Darling and the rest of them, she was melted because he had all his first teeth.

She called out to him what she had come for, and he called out to her what was she doing there; but of course neither of them understood the other's language. In fanciful stories people can talk to the birds freely, and I wish for the moment I could pretend that this was such a story, and say that Peter replied intelligently to the Never bird; but truth is best, and I want to tell only what really happened. Well, not only could they not understand each other, but they forgot their manners.

'I – want – you – to – get – into – the – nest,' the bird called, speaking as slowly and distinctly as possible, 'and – then — you – can – drift – ashore, but – I – am – too – tired – to – bring – it – any – nearer – so – you – must – try – to – swim – to – it.'

'What are you quacking about?' Peter answered. 'Why don't you let the nest drift as usual?'

'I – want – you –' the bird said, and repeated it all over.

Then Peter tried slow and distinct.

'What – are – you – quacking – about?' and so on.

The Never bird became irritated; they have very short tempers.

'You dunderheaded little jay,' she screamed, 'why don't you do as I tell you?'

Peter felt that she was calling him names, and at a venture he retorted hotly:

'So are you!'

Then rather curiously they both snapped out the same remark:

'Shut up!'

'Shut up!'

Nevertheless the bird was determined to save him if she could, and by one last mighty effort she propelled the nest against the rock. Then up she flew; deserting her eggs, so as to make her meaning clear.

Then at last he understood, and clutched the nest and waved his thanks to the bird as she fluttered overhead. It was not to receive his thanks, however, that she hung there in the sky; it was not even to watch him get into the nest; it was to see what he did with her eggs.

There were two large white eggs, and Peter lifted them up and reflected. The bird covered her face with her wings, so as not to see the last of her eggs; but she could not help peeping between the feathers.

I forget whether I have told you that there was a stave on the rock, driven into it by some buccaneers of long ago to mark the site of buried treasure. The children had discovered the glittering hoard, and when in mischievous mood used to fling showers of moidores, diamonds, pearls and pieces of eight to the gulls, who pounced upon them for food, and then flew away, raging at the scurvy trick that had been played upon them. The stave was still there, and on it Starkey had hung his hat, a deep tarpaulin, watertight, with a broad brim. Peter put the eggs into this hat and set it on the lagoon. It floated beautifully.

The Never bird saw at once what he was up to, and screamed her admiration of him; and, alas, Peter crowed his agreement with her. Then he got into the nest, reared the stave in it as a mast, and hung up his shirt for a sail. At the same moment the bird fluttered down upon the hat and once more sat snugly on her eggs. She drifted in one direction, and he was borne off in another, both cheering.

Of course when Peter landed he beached his barque in a place where the bird would easily find it; but the hat was such a great success that she abandoned the nest. It drifted about till it went to pieces, and often Starkey came to the shore of the lagoon, and with many bitter feelings, watched the bird sitting on his hat. As we shall not see her again, it may be worth mentioning here that all Never birds now build in that shape of nest, with a broad brim on which the youngsters take an airing.

Great were the rejoicings when Peter reached the home under the ground almost as soon as Wendy, who had been carried hither and thither by the kite. Every boy had adventures to tell; but perhaps the biggest adventure of all was that they were several hours late for bed. This so inflated them that they did various dodgy things to get staying up still longer, such as demanding bandages; but Wendy, though glorying in having them all home again safe and sound, was scandalized by the lateness of the hour, and cried, 'To bed, to bed,' in a voice that had to be obeyed. Next day, however, she was awfully tender, and gave out bandages to every one; and they played till bedtime at limping about and carrying their arms in slings.

10   The Happy Home

One important result of the brush on the lagoon was that it made the redskins their friends. Peter had saved Tiger Lily from a dreadful fate, and now there was nothing she and her braves would not do for him. All night they sat above, keeping watch over the home under the ground and awaiting the big attack by the pirates which obviously could not be much longer delayed. Even by day they hung about, smoking the pipe of peace, and looking almost as if they wanted tit-bits to eat.

They called Peter the Great White Father, prostrating themselves before him; and he liked this tremendously, so that it was not really good for him.

'The Great White Father,' he would say to them in a very lordly manner, as they grovelled at his feet, 'is glad to see the Piccaninny warriors protecting his wigwam from the pirates.'

'Me Tiger Lily,' that lovely creature would reply. 'Peter Pan save me, me his velly nice friend. Me no let pirates hurt him.'

She was far too pretty to cringe in this way, but Peter thought it his due, and he would answer condescendingly, 'It is good. Peter Pan has spoken.'

Always when he said 'Peter Pan has spoken', it meant that they must now shut up, and they accepted it humbly in that spirit; but they were by no means so respectful to the other boys, whom they looked upon as just ordinary braves. They said 'How-do?' to them, and things like that; and what annoyed the boys was that Peter seemed to think this all right.

Secretly Wendy sympathized with them a little, but she was far too loyal a housewife to listen to any complaints against father. 'Father knows best,' she always said, whatever her private opinion might be. Her private opinion was that the redskins should not call her squaw.

We have now reached the evening that was to be known among them as the Night of Nights, because of its adventures and their upshot. The day, as if quietly gathering its forces, had been almost uneventful, and now the redskins in their blankets were at their posts above, while, below, the children were having their evening meal; all except Peter, who had gone out to get the time. The way you got the time on the island was to find the crocodile, and then stay near him till the clock struck.

This meal happened to be a make-believe tea, and they sat round the board, guzzling in their greed; and really, what with their chatter and recriminations, the noise, as Wendy said, was positively deafening. To be sure, she did not mind noise, but she simply would not have them grabbing things, and then excusing themselves by saying that Tootles had pushed their elbow. There was a fixed rule that they must never hit back at meals, but should refer the matter of dispute to Wendy by raising the right arm politely and saying, 'I complain of So-and-so'; but what usually happened was that they forgot to do this or did it too much.

'Silence,' cried Wendy when for the twentieth time she had told them that they were not all to speak at once. 'Is your calabash empty, Slightly, darling?'

'Not quite empty, Mummy,' Slightly said, after looking into an imaginary mug.

'He hasn't even begun to drink his milk,' Nibs interposed.

This was telling, and Slightly seized his chance.

'I complain of Nibs,' he cried promptly.

John, however, had held up his hand first.

'Well, John?'

'May I sit in Peter's chair, as he is not here?'

'Sit in father's chair, John!' Wendy was scandalized. 'Certainly not.'

'He is not really our father,' John answered. 'He didn't even know how a father does till I showed him.'

This was grumbling. 'We complain of John,' cried the twins.

Tootles held up his hand. He was so much the humblest of them, indeed he was the only humble one, that Wendy was specially gentle with him.

'I don't suppose,' Tootles said diffidently, 'that I could be father.'

'No, Tootles.'

Once Tootles began, which was not very often, he had a silly way of going on.

'As I can't be father,' he said heavily, 'I don't suppose, Michael, you would let me be baby?'

'No, I won't,' Michael rapped out. He was already in his basket.

'As I can't be baby,' Tootles said, getting heavier and heavier, 'do you think I could be a twin?'

'No, indeed,' replied the twins; 'it's awfully difficult to be a twin.'

'As I can't be anything important,' said Tootles, 'would any of you like to see me do a trick?'

'No,' they all replied.

Then at last he stopped. 'I hadn't really any hope,' he said.

The hateful telling broke out again.

'Slightly is coughing on the table.'

'The twins began with mammee-apples.'

'Curly is taking both tappa rolls and yams.'

'Nibs is speaking with his mouth full.'

'I complain of the twins.'

'I complain of Curly.'

'I complain of Nibs.'

'Oh dear, oh dear,' cried Wendy, 'I'm sure I sometimes think that children are more trouble than they are worth.'

She told them to clear away, and sat down to her work-basket: a heavy load of stockings and every knee with a hole in it as usual.

'Wendy,' remonstrated Michael, 'I'm too big for a cradle.'

'I must have somebody in a cradle,' she said almost tartly, 'and you are the littlest. A cradle is such a nice homely thing to have about a house.'

While she sewed they played around her; such a group of happy faces and dancing limbs lit up by that romantic fire. It had become a very familiar scene this in the home under the ground, but we are looking on it for the last time.

There was a step above, and Wendy, you may be sure, was the first to recognize it.

'Children, I hear your father's step. He likes you to meet him at the door.'

Above, the redskins crouched before Peter.

'Watch well, braves, I have spoken.'

And then, as so often before, the gay children dragged him from his tree. As so often before, but never again.

He had brought nuts for the boys as well as the correct time for Wendy.

'Peter, you just spoil them, you know,' Wendy simpered.

'Aye, old lady,' said Peter, hanging up his gun.

'It was me told him mothers are called old lady,' Michael whispered to Curly.

'I complain of Michael,' said Curly instantly.

The first twin came to Peter. 'Father, we want to dance.'

'Dance away, my little man,' said Peter, who was in high good humour.

'But we want you to dance.'

Peter was really the best dancer among them, but he pretended to be scandalized.

'Me! My old bones would rattle.'

'And mummy too.'

'What,' cried Wendy, 'the mother of such an armful, dance!'

'But on a Saturday night,' Slightly insinuated.

It was not really Saturday night, at least it may have been, for they had long lost count of the days; but always if they wanted to do anything special they said this was Saturday night, and then they did it.

'Of course it is Saturday night, Peter,' Wendy said, relenting.

'People of our figure, Wendy.'

'But it is only among our own progeny.'

'True, true.'

So they were told they could dance, but they must put on their nighties first.

'Ah, old lady,' Peter said aside to Wendy, warming himself by the fire and looking down at her as she sat turning a heel, 'there is nothing more pleasant of an evening for you and me when the day's toil is over than to rest by the fire with the little ones near by.'

'It is sweet, Peter, isn't it?' Wendy said, frightfully gratified. 'Peter, I think Curly has your nose.'

'Michael takes after you.'

She went to him and put her hand on his shoulder.

'Dear Peter,' she said, 'with such a large family, of course, I have now passed my best, but you don't want to change me, do you?'

'No, Wendy.'

Certainly he did not want a change, but he looked at her uncomfortably; blinking, you know, like one not sure whether he was awake or asleep.

'Peter, what is it?'

'I was just thinking,' he said, a little scared. 'It is only make-believe, isn't it, that I am their father?'

'Oh yes,' Wendy said primly.

'You see,' he continued apologetically, 'it would make me seem so old to be their real father.'

'But they are ours, Peter, yours and mine.'

'But not really, Wendy?' he asked anxiously.

'Not if you don't wish it,' she replied; and she distinctly heard his sigh of relief. 'Peter,' she asked, trying to speak firmly, 'what are your exact feelings for me?'

'Those of a devoted son, Wendy.'

'I thought so,' she said, and went and sat by herself at the extreme end of the room.

'You are so queer,' he said, frankly puzzled, 'and Tiger Lily is just the same. There is something she wants to be to me, but she says it is not my mother.'

'No, indeed, it is not,' Wendy replied with frightful emphasis. Now we know why she was prejudiced against the redskins.

'Then, what is it?'

'It isn't for a lady to tell.'

'Oh, very well,' Peter said, a little nettled. 'Perhaps Tinker Bell will tell me.'

'Oh yes, Tinker Bell will tell you,' Wendy retorted scornfully. 'She is an abandoned little creature.'

Here Tink, who was in her boudoir, eavesdropping, squeaked out something impudent.

'She says she glories in being abandoned,' Peter interpreted.

He had a sudden idea. 'Perhaps Tink wants to be my mother?'

'You silly ass!' cried Tinker Bell in a passion.

She had said it so often that Wendy needed no translation.

'I almost agree with her,' Wendy snapped. Fancy Wendy snapping. But she had been much tried, and she little knew what was to happen before the night was out. If she had known she would not have snapped.

None of them knew. Perhaps it was best not to know. Their ignorance gave them one more glad hour; and as it was to be their last hour on the island, let us rejoice that there were sixty minutes in it. They sang and danced in their night-gowns. Such a deliciously creepy song it was, in which they pretended to be frightened at their own shadows; little witting that so soon shadows would close in upon them, from whom they would shrink in real fear. So uproariously gay was the dance, and how they buffeted each other on the bed and out of it! It was a pillow fight rather than a dance, and when it was finished, the pillows insisted on one bout more, like partners who know that they may never meet again. The stories they told, before it was time for Wendy's good night story! Even Slightly tried to tell a story that night, but the beginning was so fearfully dull that it appalled even himself, and he said gloomily:

'Yes, it is a dull beginning. I say, let us pretend that it is the end.'

And then at last they all got into bed for Wendy's story, the story they loved best, the story Peter hated. Usually when she began to tell this story he left the room or put his hands over his ears; and possibly if he had done either of those things this time they might all still be on the island. But tonight he remained on his stool; and we shall see what happened.

11 Wendy's Story

'Listen, then,' said Wendy, settling down to her story, with Michael at her feet and seven boys in the bed. 'There was once a gentleman –'

'I had rather he had been a lady,' Curly said.

'I wish he had been a white rat,' said Nibs.

'Quiet,' their mother admonished them. 'There was a lady also, and –'

'O Mummy,' cried the first twin, 'you mean that there is a lady also, don't you? She is not dead, is she?'

'Oh, no.'

'I am awfully glad she isn't dead,' said Tootles. 'Are you glad, John?'

'Of course I am.'

'Are you glad, Nibs?'

'Rather.'

'Are you glad, Twins?'

'We are just glad.'

'Oh dear,' sighed Wendy.

'Little less noise there,' Peter called out, determined that she should have fair play, however beastly a story it might be in his opinion.

'The gentleman's name,' Wendy continued, 'was Mr Darling, and her name was Mrs Darling.'

'I knew them,' John said, to annoy the others.

'I think I knew them,' said Michael rather doubtfully.

'They were married, you know,' explained Wendy, 'and what do you think they had?'

'White rats,' cried Nibs, inspired.

'No.'

'It's awfully puzzling,' said Tootles, who knew the story by heart.

'Quiet, Tootles. They had three descendants.'

'What is descendants?'

'Well, you are one, Twin.'

'Do you hear that, John? I am a descendant.'

'Descendants are only children,' said John.

'Oh dear, oh dear,' sighed Wendy. 'Now, these three children had a faithful nurse called Nana; but Mr Darling was angry with her and chained her up in the yard; and so all the children flew away.'

'It's an awfully good story,' said Nibs.

'They flew away,' Wendy continued, 'to the Neverland, where the lost children are.'

'I just thought they did,' Curly broke in excitedly. 'I don't know how it is, but I just thought they did.'

'O Wendy,' cried Tootles, 'was one of the lost children called Tootles?'

'Yes, he was.'

'I am in a story. Hurrah, I am in a story, Nibs.'

'Hush. Now, I want you to consider the feelings of the unhappy parents with all their children flown away.'

'Oo!' they all moaned, though they were not really considering the feelings of the unhappy parents one jot.

'Think of the empty beds!'

'Oo!'

'It's awfully sad,' the first twin said cheerfully.

'I don't see how it can have a happy ending,' said the second twin. 'Do you, Nibs?'

'I'm frightfully anxious.'

'If you knew how great is a mother's love,' Wendy told them triumphantly, 'you would have no fear.' She had now come to the part that Peter hated.

'I do like a mother's love,' said Tootles, hitting Nibs with a pillow. 'Do you like a mother's love, Nibs?'

'I do just,' said Nibs, hitting back.

'You see,' Wendy said complacently, 'our heroine knew that the mother would always leave the window open for her children to fly back by; so they stayed away for years and had a lovely time.'

'Did they ever go back?'

'Let us now,' said Wendy, bracing herself for her finest effort, 'take a peep into the future'; and they all gave themselves the twist that makes peeps into the future easier. 'Years have rolled by; and who is this elegant lady of uncertain age alighting at London Station?'

'O Wendy, who is she?' cried Nibs, every bit as excited as if he didn't know.

'Can it be – yes – no – it is – the fair Wendy!'

'Oh!'

'And who are the two noble portly figures accompanying her, now grown to man's estate? Can they be John and Michael? They are!'

'Oh!'

' "See, dear brothers," says Wendy, pointing upwards, "there is the window still standing open. Ah, now we are rewarded for our sublime faith in a mother's love." So up they flew to their mummy and daddy; and pen cannot describe the happy scene, over which we draw a veil.'

That was a story, and they were as pleased with it as the fair narrator herself. Everything just as it should be, you see. Off we skip like the most heartless things in the world, which is what children are, but so attractive; and we have an entirely selfish time; and then when we have need of special attention we nobly return for it, confident that we shall be embraced instead of smacked.

So great indeed was their faith in a mother's love that they felt they could afford to be callous for a bit longer.

But there was one there who knew better; and when Wendy finished he uttered a hollow groan.

'What is it, Peter?' she cried, running to him, thinking he was ill. She felt him solicitously, lower down than his chest. 'Where is it, Peter?'

'It isn't that kind of pain,' Peter replied darkly.

'Then what kind is it?'

'Wendy, you are wrong about mothers.'

They all gathered round him in affright, so alarming was his agitation; and with a fine candour he told them what he had hitherto concealed.

'Long ago,' he said, 'I thought like you that my mother would always keep the window open for me; so I stayed away for moons and moons and moons, and then flew back; but the window was barred, for mother had forgotten all about me, and there was another little boy sleeping in my bed.'

I am not sure that this was true, but Peter thought it was true; and it scared them.

'Are you sure mothers are like that?'

'Yes.'

So this was the truth about mothers. The toads!

Still it is best to be careful; and no one knows so quickly as a child when he should give in. 'Wendy, let us go home,' cried John and Michael together.

'Yes,' she said, clutching them.

'Not tonight?' asked the lost boys bewildered. They knew in what they called their hearts that one can get on quite well without a mother, and that it is only the mothers who think you can't.

'At once,' Wendy replied resolutely, for the horrible thought had come to her: 'Perhaps mother is in half-mourning by this time.'

This dread made her forgetful of what must be Peter's feelings, and she said to him rather sharply, 'Peter, will you make the necessary arrangements?'

'If you wish it,' he replied as coolly as if she had asked him to pass the nuts.

Not so much as a sorry-to-lose-you between them! If she did not mind the parting, he was going to show her, was Peter, that neither did he.

But of course he cared very much; and he was so full of wrath against grown-ups, who, as usual, were spoiling everything, that as soon as he got inside his tree he breathed intentionally quick short breaths at the rate of about five to a second. He did this because there is a saying in the Neverland that every time you breathe, a grown-up dies; and Peter was killing them off vindictively as fast as possible.

Then having given the necessary instructions to the redskins he returned to the home, where an unworthy scene had been enacted in his absence. Panic-stricken at the thought of losing Wendy, the lost boys had advanced upon her threateningly.

'It will be worse than before she came,' they cried.

'We shan't let her go.'

'Let's keep her prisoner.'

'Aye, chain her up.'

In her extremity an instinct told her to which of them to turn.

'Tootles,' she cried, 'I appeal to you.'

Was it not strange? She appealed to Tootles, quite the silliest one.

Grandly, however, did Tootles respond. For that one moment he dropped his silliness and spoke with dignity.

'I am just Tootles,' he said, 'and nobody minds me. But the first who does not behave to Wendy like an English gentleman I will blood him severely.'

He drew his hangar; and for that instant his sun was at noon. The others held back uneasily. Then Peter returned, and they saw at once that they would get no support from him. He would keep no girl in the Neverland against her will.

'Wendy,' he said, striding up and down, 'I have asked the redskins to guide you through the wood, as flying tires you so.'

'Thank you, Peter.'

'Then,' he continued in the short sharp voice of one accustomed to be obeyed, 'Tinker Bell will take you across the sea. Wake her, Nibs.'

Nibs had to knock twice before he got an answer, though Tink had really been sitting up in bed listening for some time.

'Who are you? How dare you? Go away,' she cried.

'You are to get up, Tink,' Nibs called, 'and take Wendy on a journey.'

Of course Tink had been delighted to hear that Wendy was going; but she was jolly well determined not to be her courier, and she said so in still more offensive language. Then she pretended to be asleep again.

'She says she won't,' Nibs exclaimed, aghast at such insubordination, whereupon Peter went sternly towards the young lady's chamber.

'Tink,' he rapped out, 'if you don't get up and dress at once I will open the curtains, and then we shall all see you in your *négligé*.'

This made her leap to the floor. 'Who said I wasn't getting up?' she cried.

In the meantime the boys were gazing very forlornly at Wendy, now equipped with John and Michael for the journey. By this time they were dejected, not merely because they were about to lose her, but also because they felt that she was going off to something nice to which they had not been invited. Novelty was beckoning to them as usual.

Crediting them with a nobler feeling, Wendy melted.

'Dear ones,' she said, 'if you will all come with me I feel almost sure I can get my father and mother to adopt you.'

The invitation was meant specially for Peter; but each of the boys was thinking exclusively of himself, and at once they jumped with joy.

'But won't they think us rather a handful?' Nibs asked in the middle of his jump.

'Oh, no,' said Wendy, rapidly thinking it out, 'it will only mean having a few beds in the drawing-room; they can be hidden behind screens on first Thursdays.'

'Peter, can we go?' they all cried imploringly. They took it for granted that if they went he would go also, but really they scarcely cared. Thus children are ever ready, when novelty knocks, to desert their dearest ones.

'All right,' Peter replied with a bitter smile; and immediately they rushed to get their things.

'And now, Peter,' Wendy said, thinking she had put everything right, 'I am going to give you your medicine before you go.' She loved to give them medicine, and undoubtedly gave them too much. Of course it was only water, but it was out of a calabash, and she always shook the calabash and counted the drops, which gave it a certain medicinal quality. On this occasion, however, she did not give Peter this draught, for just as she had prepared it, she saw a look on his face that made her heart sink.

'Get your things, Peter,' she cried, shaking.

'No,' he answered, pretending indifference, 'I am not going with you, Wendy.'

'Yes, Peter.'

'No.'

To show that her departure would leave him unmoved, he skipped up and down the room, playing gaily on his heartless pipes. She had to run about after him, though it was rather undignified.

'To find your mother,' she coaxed.

Now, if Peter had ever quite had a mother, he no longer missed her. He could do very well without one. He had thought them out, and remembered only their bad points.

'No, no,' he told Wendy decisively; 'perhaps she

would say I was old, and I just want always to be a little boy and to have fun.'

'But, Peter –'

'No.'

And so the others had to be told.

'Peter isn't coming.'

Peter not coming! They gazed blankly at him, their sticks over their backs, and on each stick a bundle. Their first thought was that if Peter was not going he had prob-ably changed his mind about letting them go.

But he was far too proud for that. 'If you find your mothers,' he said darkly, 'I hope you will like them.'

The awful cynicism of this made an uncomfortable im-pression, and most of them began to look rather doubtful. After all, their faces said, were they not noodles to want to go?

'Now then,' cried Peter, 'no fuss, no blubbering; good-bye, Wendy'; and he held out his hand cheerily, quite as if they must really go now, for he had something important to do.

She had to take his hand, as there was no indication that he would prefer a thimble.

'You will remember about changing your flannels, Peter?' she said, lingering over him. She was always so particular about their flannels.

'Yes.'

'And you will take your medicine?'

'Yes.'

That seemed to be everything; and an awkward pause followed. Peter, however, was not the kind that breaks down before people. 'Are you ready, Tinker Bell?' he called out.

'Aye, aye.'

'Then lead the way.'

Tink darted up the nearest tree; but no one followed

her, for it was at this moment that the pirates made their
dreadful attack upon the redskins. Above, where all had
been so still, the air was rent with shrieks and the clash
of steel. Below, there was dead silence. Mouths opened
and remained open. Wendy fell on her knees, but her
arms were extended towards Peter. All arms were extended to him, as if suddenly blown in his direction; they
were beseeching him mutely not to desert them. As for
Peter, he seized his sword, the same he thought he had
slain Barbecue with; and the lust of battle was in his eye.

12 The Children are Carried Off

The pirate attack had been a complete surprise; a sure proof that the unscrupulous Hook had conducted it improperly, for to surprise redskins fairly is beyond the wit of the white man.

By all the unwritten laws of savage warfare it is always the redskin who attacks, and with the wiliness of his race he does it just before the dawn, at which time he knows the courage of the whites to be at its lowest ebb. The white men have in the meantime made a rude stockade on the summit of yonder undulating ground, at the foot of which a stream runs; for it is destruction to be too far from water. There they await the onslaught, the inexperienced ones clutching their revolvers and treading on twigs, but the old hands sleeping tranquilly until just before the dawn. Through the long black night the savage scouts wriggle, snake-like, among the grass without stirring a blade. The brushwood closes behind them as silently as sand into which a mole has dived. Not a sound is to be heard, save when they give vent to a wonderful imitation of the lonely call of the coyote. The cry is answered by other braves; and some of them do it even better than the coyotes, who are not very good at it. So the chill hours wear on, and the long suspense is horribly trying to the paleface who has to live through it for the first time; but to the trained hand those ghastly calls and still ghastlier silences are but an intimation of how the night is marching.

That this was the usual procedure was so well known to Hook that in disregarding it he cannot be excused on the pleas of ignorance.

The Piccaninnies, on their part, trusted implicitly to his honour, and their whole action of the night stands out in marked contrast to his. They left nothing undone that was consistent with the reputation of their tribe. With that alertness of the senses which is at once the marvel and despair of civilized peoples, they knew that the pirates were on the island from the moment one of them trod on a dry stick; and in an incredibly short space of time the coyote cries began. Every foot of ground between the spot where Hook had landed his forces and the home under the trees was stealthily examined by braves wearing their moccasins with the heels in front. They found only one hillock with a stream at its base, so that Hook had no choice; here he must establish himself and wait for just before the dawn. Everything being thus mapped out with almost diabolical cunning, the main body of the redskins folded their blankets around them, and in the phlegmatic manner that is to them the pearl of manhood squatted above the children's home, awaiting the cold moment when they should deal pale death.

Here dreaming, though wide awake, of the exquisite tortures to which they were to put him at break of day, those confiding savages were found by the treacherous Hook. From the accounts afterwards supplied by such of the scouts as escaped the carnage, he does not seem even to have paused at the rising ground, though it is certain that in that grey light he must have seen it: no thought of waiting to be attacked appears from first to last to have visited his subtle mind; he would not even hold off till the night was nearly spent; on he pounded with no policy but to fall to. What could the bewildered scouts do, masters as they were of every warlike artifice save this one, but trot helplessly after him, exposing themselves fatally to view, the while they gave pathetic utterance to the coyote cry.

Around the brave Tiger Lily were a dozen of her stoutest warriors, and they suddenly saw the perfidious pirates bearing down upon them. Fell from their eyes then the film through which they had looked at victory. No more would they torture at the stake. For them the happy hunting-grounds now. They knew it; but as their fathers' sons they acquitted themselves. Even then they had time to gather in a phalanx that would have been hard to break had they risen quickly, but this they were forbidden to do by the traditions of their race. It is written that the noble savage must never express surprise in the presence of the white. Thus terrible as the sudden appearance of the pirates must have been to them, they remained stationary for a moment, not a muscle moving; as if the foe had come by invitation. Then, indeed, the tradition gallantly upheld, they seized their weapons, and the air was torn with the war-cry; but it was now too late.

It is no part of ours to describe what was a massacre rather than a fight. Thus perished many of the flower of the Piccaninny tribe. Not all unavenged did they die, for with Lean Wolf fell Alf Mason, to disturb the Spanish Main no more; and among others who bit the dust were Geo. Scourie, Chas. Turley, and the Alsatian Foggerty. Turley fell to the tomahawk of the terrible Panther, who ultimately cut a way through the pirates with Tiger Lily and a small remnant of the tribe.

To what extent Hook is to blame for his tactics on this occasion is for the historian to decide. Had he waited on the rising ground till the proper hour he and his men would probably have been butchered; and in judging him it is only fair to take this into account. What he should perhaps have done was to acquaint his opponents that he proposed to follow a new method. On the other hand this, as destroying the element of surprise, would have made his strategy of no avail, so that the whole question is beset with difficulties. One cannot at least withhold a reluctant admiration for the wit that had conceived so bold a scheme, and the fell genius with which it was carried out.

What were his own feelings about himself at that triumphant moment? Fain would his dogs have known, as breathing heavily and wiping their cutlasses, they gathered at a discreet distance from his hook, and squinted through their ferret eyes at this extraordinary man. Elation must have been in his heart, but his face did not reflect it: ever a dark and solitary enigma, he stood aloof from his followers in spirit as in substance.

The night's work was not yet over, for it was not the redskins he had come out to destroy; they were but the bees to be smoked, so that he should get at the honey. It was Pan he wanted, Pan and Wendy and their band, but chiefly Pan.

Peter was such a small boy that one tends to wonder at the man's hatred of him. True, he had flung Hook's arm to the crocodile; but even this and the increased insecurity of life to which it led, owing to the crocodile's pertinacity, hardly account for a vindictiveness so relentless and malignant. The truth is that there was a something about Peter which goaded the pirate captain to frenzy. It was not his courage, it was not his engaging appearance, it was not – There is no beating about the bush, for we know quite well what it was, and have got to tell. It was Peter's cockiness.

This had got on Hook's nerves; it made his iron claw twitch, and at night it disturbed him like an insect. While Peter lived, the tortured man felt that he was a lion in a cage into which a sparrow had come.

The question now was how to get down the trees, or how to get his dogs down. He ran his greedy eyes over them, searching for the thinnest ones. They wriggled uncomfortably, for they knew that he would not scruple to ram them down with poles.

In the meantime, what of the boys? We have seen them at the first clang of weapons, turned as it were into stone figures, open-mouthed, all appealing with outstretched arms to Peter; and we return to them as their mouths close, and their arms fall to their sides. The pandemonium above has ceased almost as suddenly as it arose, passed like a fierce gust of wind; but they know that in the passing it has determined their fate.

Which side had won?

The pirates, listening avidly at the mouths of the trees, heard the question put by every boy, and alas! they also heard Peter's answer.

'If the redskins have won,' he said, 'they will beat the tom-tom; it is always their sign of victory.'

Now Smee had found the tom-tom, and was at that moment sitting on it. 'You will never hear the tom-tom again,' he muttered, but inaudibly of course, for strict silence had been enjoined. To his amazement Hook signed to him to beat the tom-tom; and slowly there came to Smee an understanding of the dreadful wickedness of the order. Never, probably, had this simple man admired Hook so much.

Twice Smee beat upon the instrument, and then stopped to listen gleefully.

'The tom-tom,' the miscreants heard Peter cry; 'an Indian victory!'

The doomed children answered with a cheer that was music to the black hearts above, and almost immediately they repeated their good-byes to Peter. This puzzled the pirates, but all their other feelings were swallowed by a base delight that the enemy were about to come up the trees. They smirked at each other and rubbed their hands. Rapidly and silently Hook gave his orders: one man to each tree, and the others to arrange themselves in a line two yards apart.

13 Do You Believe in Fairies?

The more quickly this horror is disposed of the better. The first to emerge from his tree was Curly. He rose out of it into the arms of Cecco, who flung him to Smee, who flung him to Starkey, who flung him to Bill Jukes, who flung him to Noodler, and so he was tossed from one to another till he fell at the feet of the black pirate. All the boys were plucked from their trees in this ruthless manner; and several of them were in the air at a time, like bales of goods flung from hand to hand.

A different treatment was accorded to Wendy, who came last. With ironical politeness Hook raised his hat to her, and, offering her his arm, escorted her to the spot where the others were being gagged. He did it with such an air, he was so frightfully *distingué*, that she was too fascinated to cry out. She was only a little girl.

Perhaps it is tell-tale to divulge that for a moment Hook entranced her, and we tell on her only because her slip led to strange results. Had she haughtily unhanded him (and we should have loved to write it of her), she would have been hurled through the air like the others, and then Hook would probably not have been present at the tying of the children; and had he not been at the tying he would not have discovered Slightly's secret, and without the secret he could not presently have made his foul attempt on Peter's life.

They were tied to prevent their flying away, doubled up with their knees close to their ears; and for the trussing of them the black pirate had cut a rope into nine equal pieces. All went well until Slightly's turn came, when he was found to be like those irritating parcels that use up all the string in going round and leave no tags with which to tie a knot. The pirates kicked him in their rage, just as you kick the parcel (though in fairness you should kick the string); and strange to say it was Hook who told them to belay their violence. His lip was curled with malicious triumph. While his dogs were merely sweating because every time they tried to pack the unhappy lad tight in one part he bulged out in another, Hook's master mind had gone far beneath Slightly's surface, probing not for effects but for causes; and his exultation showed that he had found them. Slightly, white to the gills, knew that Hook had surprised his secret, which was this, that no boy so blown out would use a tree wherein an average man need stick. Poor Slightly, most wretched of all the children now, for he was in a panic about Peter, bitterly regretted what he had done. Madly addicted to the drinking of water when he was hot, he had swelled in consequence to his present girth, and instead of reducing

himself to fit his tree had, unknown to the others, whittled
his tree to make it fit him.

Sufficient of this Hook guessed to persuade him that
Peter at last lay at his mercy; but no word of the dark
design that now formed in the subterranean caverns of
his mind crossed his lips; he merely signed that the
captives were to be conveyed to the ship, and that he
would be alone.

How to convey them? Hunched up in their ropes they
might indeed be rolled downhill like barrels, but most of
the way lay through a morass. Again Hook's genius sur-
mounted difficulties. He indicated that the little house
must be used as a conveyance. The children were flung
into it, four stout pirates raised it on their shoulders, the
others fell in behind, and singing the hateful pirate chorus

the strange procession set off through the wood. I don't know whether any of the children were crying; if so, the singing drowned the sound; but as the little house disappeared in the forest, a brave though tiny jet of smoke issued from its chimney as if defying Hook.

Hook saw it, and it did Peter a bad service. It dried up any trickle of pity for him that may have remained in the pirate's infuriated breast.

The first thing he did on finding himself alone in the fast-falling night was to tiptoe to Slightly's tree, and make sure that it provided him with a passage. Then for long he remained brooding; his hat of ill omen on the sward, so that a gentle breeze which had arisen might play refreshingly through his hair. Dark as were his thoughts his blue eyes were as soft as the periwinkle. Intently he listened for any sound from the nether world, but all was as silent below as above; the house under the ground seemed to be but one more empty tenement in the void. Was that boy asleep, or did he stand waiting at the foot of Slightly's tree, with his dagger in his hand?

There was no way of knowing, save by going down. Hook let his cloak slip softly to the ground, and then biting his lips till a lewd blood stood on them, he stepped into the tree. He was a brave man; but for a moment he had to stop there and wipe his brow, which was dripping like a candle. Then silently he let himself go into the unknown.

He arrived unmolested at the foot of the shaft, and stood still again, biting at his breath, which had almost left him. As his eyes became accustomed to the dim light various objects in the home under the trees took shape; but the only one on which his greedy gaze rested, long sought for and found at last, was the great bed. On the bed lay Peter fast asleep.

Unaware of the tragedy being enacted above, Peter had

continued, for a little time after the children left, to play gaily on his pipes: no doubt rather a forlorn attempt to prove to himself that he did not care. Then he decided not to take his medicine, so as to grieve Wendy. Then he lay down on the bed outside the coverlet, to vex her still more; for she had always tucked them inside it, because you never know that you may not grow chilly at the turn of the night. Then he nearly cried; but it struck him how indignant she would be if he laughed instead; so he laughed a haughty laugh and fell asleep in the middle of it.

Sometimes, though not often, he had dreams, and they were more painful than the dreams of other boys. For hours he could not be separated from these dreams, though he wailed piteously in them. They had to do, I think, with the riddle of his existence. At such times it had been Wendy's custom to take him out of bed and sit with him on her lap, soothing him in dear ways of her own invention, and when he grew calmer to put him back to bed before he quite woke up, so that he should not know of the indignity to which she had subjected him. But on this occasion he had fallen at once into a dreamless sleep. One arm dropped over the edge of the bed, one leg was arched, and the unfinished part of his laugh was stranded on his mouth, which was open, showing the little pearls.

Thus defenceless, Hook found him. He stood silent at the foot of the tree looking across the chamber at his enemy. Did no feeling of compassion disturb his sombre breast? The man was not wholly evil; he loved flowers (I have been told) and sweet music (he was himself no mean performer on the harpsichord); and let it be frankly admitted, the idyllic nature of the scene stirred him profoundly. Mastered by his better self, he would have returned reluctantly up the tree but for one thing.

What stayed him was Peter's impertinent appearance as he slept. The open mouth, the drooping arm, the arched knee: they were such a personification of cockiness as, taken together, will never again, one may hope, be presented to eyes so sensitive to their offensiveness. They steeled Hook's heart. If his rage had broken him into a hundred pieces every one of them would have disregarded the incident, and leapt at the sleeper.

Though a light from the one lamp shone dimly on the bed Hook stood in darkness himself, and at the first stealthy step forward he discovered an obstacle, the door of Slightly's tree. It did not entirely fill the aperture, and he had been looking over it. Feeling for the catch, he found to his fury that it was low down, beyond his reach. To his disordered brain it seemed then that the irritating quality in Peter's face and figure visibly increased, and he rattled the door and flung himself against it. Was his enemy to escape him after all ?

But what was that ? The red in his eye had caught sight of Peter's medicine standing on a ledge within easy reach. He fathomed what it was straightway, and immediately he knew that the sleeper was in his power.

Lest he should be taken alive, Hook always carried about his person a dreadful drug, blended by himself of all the death-dealing rings that had come into his possession. These he had boiled down into a yellow liquid quite unknown to science, which was probably the most virulent poison in existence.

Five drops of this he now added to Peter's cup. His hand shook, but it was in exultation rather than in shame. As he did it he avoided glancing at the sleeper, but not lest pity should unnerve him; merely to avoid spilling. Then one long gloating look he cast upon his victim, and turning, wormed his way with difficulty up the tree. As he emerged at the top he looked the very spirit of evil

breaking from its hole. Donning his hat at its most rakish
angle, he wound his cloak around him, holding one end
in front as if to conceal his person from the night, of
which it was the blackest part, and muttering strangely
to himself stole away through the trees.

Peter slept on. The light guttered and went out, leaving the tenement in darkness; but still he slept. It must have been not less than ten o'clock by the crocodile, when he suddenly sat up in his bed, wakened by he knew not what. It was a soft cautious tapping on the door of his tree.

Soft and cautious, but in that stillness it was sinister. Peter felt for his dagger till his hand gripped it. Then he spoke.

'Who is that?'

For long there was no answer: then again the knock.

'Who are you?'

No answer.

He was thrilled, and he loved being thrilled. In two strides he reached his door. Unlike Slightly's door it filled the aperture, so that he could not see beyond it, nor could the one knocking see him.

'I won't open unless you speak,' Peter cried.

Then at last the visitor spoke, in a lovely bell-like voice.

'Let me in, Peter.'

It was Tink, and quickly he unbarred to her. She flew in excitedly, her face flushed and her dress stained with mud.

'What is it?'

'Oh, you could never guess,' she cried, and offered him three guesses. 'Out with it!' he shouted; and in one ungrammatical sentence, as long as the ribbons conjurers pull from their mouths, she told of the capture of Wendy and the boys.

Peter's heart bobbed up and down as he listened. Wendy bound, and on the pirate ship; she who loved everything to be just so!

'I'll rescue her,' he cried, leaping at his weapons. As he leapt he thought of something he could do to please her. He could take his medicine.

His hand closed on the fatal draught.

'No!' shrieked Tinker Bell, who had heard Hook muttering about his deed as he sped through the forest.

'Why not?'

'It is poisoned.'

'Poisoned? Who could have poisoned it?'

'Hook.'

'Don't be silly. How could Hook have got down here?'

Alas! Tinker Bell could not explain this, for even she did not know the dark secret of Slightly's tree. Nevertheless Hook's words had left no room for doubt. The cup was poisoned.

'Besides,' said Peter, quite believing himself, 'I never fell asleep.'

He raised the cup. No time for words now; time for deeds: and with one of her lightning movements Tink got between his lips and the draught, and drained it to the dregs.

'Why, Tink, how dare you drink my medicine?'

But she did not answer. Already she was reeling in the air.

'What is the matter with you?' cried Peter, suddenly afraid.

'It was poisoned, Peter,' she told him softly; 'and now I am going to be dead.'

'O Tink, did you drink it to save me?'

'Yes.'

'But why, Tink?'

Her wings would scarcely carry her now, but in reply she alighted on his shoulder and gave his chin a loving bite. She whispered in his ear, 'You silly ass'; and then, tottering to her chamber, lay down on the bed.

His head almost filled the fourth wall of her little room as he knelt near her in distress. Every moment her light was growing fainter; and he knew that if it went out she would be no more. She liked his tears so much that she put out her beautiful finger and let them run over it.

Her voice was so low that at first he could not make out what she said. Then he made it out. She was saying that she thought she could get well again if children believed in fairies.

Peter flung out his arms. There were no children there, and it was night-time; but he addressed all who might be dreaming of the Neverland, and who were therefore nearer to him than you think; boys and girls in their nighties, and naked papooses in their baskets hung from trees.

'Do you believe?' he cried.

Tink sat up in bed almost briskly to listen to her fate.

She fancied she heard answers in the affirmative, and then again she wasn't sure.

'What do you think?' she asked Peter.

'If you believe,' he shouted to them, 'clap your hands; don't let Tink die.'

Many clapped.

Some didn't.

A few little beasts hissed.

The clapping stopped suddenly, as if countless mothers had rushed to their nurseries to see what on earth was happening; but already Tink was saved. First her voice

grew strong; then she popped out of bed; then she was flashing through the room more merry and impudent than ever. She never thought of thanking those who believed, but she would have liked to get at the ones who had hissed.

'And now to rescue Wendy.'

The moon was riding in a cloudy heaven when Peter rose from his tree, begirt with weapons and wearing little else, to set out upon his perilous quest. It was not such a night as he would have chosen. He had hoped to fly, keeping not far from the ground so that nothing un-wonted should escape his eyes; but in that fitful light to have flown low would have meant trailing his shadow through the trees, thus disturbing the birds and acquainting a watchful foe that he was astir.

He regretted now that he had given the birds of the island such strange names that they are very wild and difficult of approach.

There was no other course but to press forward in redskin fashion, at which happily he was an adept. But in what direction, for he could not be sure that the children had been taken to the ship? A slight fall of snow had obliterated all footmarks; and a deathly silence pervaded the island, as if for a space Nature stood still in horror of the recent carnage. He had taught the children something of the forest lore that he had himself learned from Tiger Lily and Tinker Bell, and knew that in their dire hour they were not likely to forget it. Slightly, if he had an opportunity, would blaze the trees, for instance, Curly would drop seeds, and Wendy would leave her handker-chief at some important place. But morning was needed to search for such guidance, and he could not wait. The upper world had called him, but would give no help.

The crocodile passed him, but not another living thing, not a sound, not a movement; and yet he knew well that sudden death might be at the next tree, or stalking him from behind.

He swore this terrible oath: 'Hook or me this time.'

Now he crawled forward like a snake; and again, erect, he darted across a space on which the moonlight played: one finger on his lip and his dagger at the ready. He was frightfully happy.

14 The Pirate Ship

One green light squinting over Kidd's Creek, which is near the mouth of the pirate river, marked where the brig, the *Jolly Roger*, lay, low in the water; a rakish-looking craft foul to the hull, every beam in her detestable, like ground strewn with mangled feathers. She was the cannibal of the seas, and scarce needed that watchful eye, for she floated immune in the horror of her name.

She was wrapped in the blanket of night, through which no sound from her could have reached the shore. There was little sound, and none agreeable save the whir of the ship's sewing machine at which Smee sat, ever industrious and obliging, the essence of the commonplace, pathetic Smee. I know not why he was so infinitely pathetic, unless it were because he was so pathetically unaware of it; but even strong men had to turn hastily from looking at him, and more than once on summer evenings he had touched the fount of Hook's tears and made it flow. Of this, as of almost everything else, Smee was quite unconscious.

A few of the pirates leant over the bulwarks drinking in the miasma of the night; others sprawled by barrels over games of dice and cards; and the exhausted four who had carried the little house lay prone on the deck, where even in their sleep they rolled skilfully to this side or that out of Hook's reach, lest he should claw them mechanically in passing.

Hook trod the deck in thought. O man unfathomable. It was his hour of triumph. Peter had been removed for ever from his path, and all the other boys were on the brig, about to walk the plank. It was his grimmest deed since the days when he had brought Barbecue to heel; and knowing as we do how vain a tabernacle is man, could we be surprised had he now paced the deck unsteadily, bellied out by the winds of his success?

But there was no elation in his gait, which kept pace with the action of his sombre mind. Hook was profoundly dejected.

He was often thus when communing with himself on board ship in the quietude of the night. It was because he was so terribly alone. This inscrutable man never felt more alone than when surrounded by his dogs. They were socially so inferior to him.

Hook was not his true name. To reveal who he really was would even at this date set the country in a blaze; but as those who read between the lines must already have guessed, he had been at a famous public school; and its traditions still clung to him like garments, with which indeed they are largely concerned. Thus it was offensive to him even now to board a ship in the same dress in which he grappled her; and he still adhered in his walk to the school's distinguished slouch. But above all he retained the passion for good form.

Good form! However much he may have degenerated, he still knew that this is all that really matters.

From far within him he heard a creaking as of rusty portals, and through them came a stern tap-tap-tap, like hammering in the night when one cannot sleep. 'Have you been good form today?' was their eternal question.

'Fame, fame, that glittering bauble, it is mine,' he cried.

'Is it quite good form to be distinguished at anything?' the tap-tap from his school replied.

'I am the only man whom Barbecue feared,' he urged; 'and Flint himself feared Barbecue.'

'Barbecue, Flint – what house?' came the cutting retort.

Most disquieting reflection of all, was it not bad form to think about good form?

His vitals were tortured by this problem. It was a claw within him sharper than the iron one; and as it tore him, the perspiration dripped down his sallow countenance and streaked his doublet. Oft-times he drew his sleeve across his face, but there was no damming that trickle.

Ah, envy not Hook.

There came to him a presentiment of his early dissolution. It was as if Peter's terrible oath had boarded the ship. Hook felt a gloomy desire to make his dying speech, lest presently there should be no time for it.

'Better for Hook,' he cried, 'if he had had less ambition.' It was in his darkest hours only that he referred to himself in the third person.

'No little children love me.'

Strange that he should think of this, which had never troubled him before; perhaps the sewing machine brought it to his mind. For long he muttered to himself, staring at Smee, who was hemming placidly, under the conviction that all children feared him.

Feared him! Feared Smee! There was not a child on board the brig that night who did not already love him. He had said horrid things to them and hit them with the palm of his hand, because he could not hit with his fist; but they had only clung to him the more. Michael had tried on his spectacles.

To tell poor Smee that they thought him lovable! Hook itched to do it, but it seemed too brutal. Instead, he revolved this mystery in his mind: why do they find Smee lovable? He pursued the problem like the sleuth-hound that he was. If Smee was lovable, what was it that made him so? A terrible answer suddenly presented itself: 'Good form?'

Had the bo'sun good form without knowing it, which is the best form of all?

He remembered that you have to prove you don't know you have it before you are eligible for Pop.

With a cry of rage he raised his iron hand over Smee's head; but he did not tear. What arrested him was this reflection:

'To claw a man because he is good form, what would that be?'

'Bad form!'

The unhappy Hook was as impotent as he was damp, and he fell forward like a cut flower.

His dogs thinking him out of the way for a time, discipline instantly relaxed; and they broke into a bacchanalian dance, which brought him to his feet at once; all traces of human weakness gone, as if a bucket of water had passed over him.

'Quiet, you scugs,' he cried, 'or I'll cast anchor in you': and at once the din was hushed. 'Are all the children chained, so they cannot fly away?'

'Aye, aye.'

'Then hoist them up.'

The wretched prisoners were dragged from the hold, all except Wendy, and ranged in line in front of him. For a time he seemed unconscious of their presence. He lolled at his ease, humming, not unmelodiously, snatches of a rude song, and fingering a pack of cards. Ever and anon the light from his cigar gave a touch of colour to his face.

'Now then, bullies,' he said briskly, 'six of you walk the plank tonight, but I have room for two cabin boys. Which of you is it to be?'

'Don't irritate him unnecessarily,' had been Wendy's instructions in the hold; so Tootles stepped forward politely. Tootles hated the idea of signing under such a man, but an instinct told him that it would be prudent to lay responsibility on an absent person; and though a somewhat silly boy, he knew that mothers alone are always willing to be the buffer. All children know this about mothers, and despise them for it, but make constant use of it.

So Tootles explained prudently, 'You see, sir, I don't think my mother would like me to be a pirate. Would your mother like you to be a pirate, Slightly?'

He winked at Slightly, who said mournfully, 'I don't think so,' as if he wished things had been otherwise. 'Would your mother like you to be a pirate, Twin?'

'I don't think so,' said the first twin, as clever as the others. 'Nibs, would –?'

'Stow this gab,' roared Hook, and the spokesmen were dragged back. 'You, boy,' he said, addressing John, 'you look as if you had a little pluck in you. Didst never want to be a pirate, my hearty?'

Now John had sometimes experienced this hankering at maths. prep.; and he was struck by Hook's picking him out.

'I once thought of calling myself Red-handed Jack,' he said diffidently.

'And a good name too. We'll call you that here, bully, if you join.'

'What do you think, Michael?' asked John.

'What would you call me if I join?' Michael demanded.

'Blackbeard Joe.'

Michael was naturally impressed. 'What do you think, John?' He wanted John to decide, and John wanted him to decide.

'Shall we still be respectful subjects of the King?' John inquired.

Through Hook's teeth came the answer: 'You would have to swear, "Down with the King."'

Perhaps John had not behaved very well so far, but he shone out now.

'Then I refuse,' he cried, banging the barrel in front of Hook.

'And I refuse,' cried Michael.

'Rule Britannia!' squeaked Curly.

The infuriated pirates buffeted them in the mouth; and Hook roared out, 'That seals your doom. Bring up their mother. Get the plank ready.'

They were only boys, and they went white as they saw Jukes and Cecco preparing the fatal plank. But they tried to look brave when Wendy was brought up.

No words of mine can tell you how Wendy despised those pirates. To the boys there was at least some glamour in the pirate calling, but all that she saw was that the ship had not been scrubbed for years. There was not a port-hole on the grimy glass of which you might not have written with your finger. 'Dirty pig'; and she had already written it on several. But as the boys gathered round her she had no thought, of course, save for them.

'So, my beauty,' said Hook, as if he spoke in syrup, 'you are to see your children walk the plank.'

Fine gentleman though he was, the intensity of his communings had soiled his ruff, and suddenly he knew that she was gazing at it. With a hasty gesture he tried to hide it, but he was too late.

'Are they to die?' asked Wendy, with a look of such frightful contempt that he nearly fainted.

'They are,' he snarled. 'Silence all,' he called gloatingly, 'for a mother's last words to her children.'

At this moment Wendy was grand. 'These are my last words, dear boys,' she said firmly. 'I feel that I have a message to you from your real mothers, and it is this: "We hope our sons will die like English gentlemen."'

Even the pirates were awed; and Tootles cried out hysterically, 'I am going to do what my mother hopes. What are you to do, Nibs?'

'What my mother hopes. What are you to do, Twin?'

'What my mother hopes, John, what are –?'

But Hook had found his voice again.

'Tie her up,' he shouted.

It was Smee who tied her to the mast. 'See here, honey,' he whispered, 'I'll save you if you promise to be my mother.'

'But not even for Smee would she make such a promise. 'I would almost rather have no children at all,' she said disdainfully.

It is sad to know that not a boy was looking at her as

Smee tied her to the mast; the eyes of all were on the plank; that last little walk they were about to take. They were no longer able to hope that they would walk it manfully, for the capacity to think had gone from them; they could stare and shiver only.

Hook smiled on them with his teeth closed, and took a step towards Wendy. His intention was to turn her face so that she should see the boys walking the plank one by one. But he never reached her, he never heard the cry of anguish he hoped to wring from her. He heard something else instead.

It was the terrible tick-tick of the crocodile.

They all heard it – pirates, boys, Wendy; and immediately every head was blown in one direction; not to the water whence the sound proceeded, but towards Hook. All knew that what was about to happen concerned him alone, and that from being actors they were suddenly become spectators.

Very frightful was it to see the change that came over him. It was as if he had been clipped at every joint. He fell in a little heap.

The sound came steadily nearer; and in advance of it came this ghastly thought, 'The crocodile is about to board the ship.'

Even the iron claw hung inactive; as if knowing that it was no intrinsic part of what the attacking force wanted. Left so fearfully alone, any other man would have lain with his eyes shut where he fell: but the gigantic brain of Hook was still working, and under its guidance he crawled on his knees along the deck as far from the sound as he could go. The pirates respectfully cleared a passage for him, and it was only when he brought up against the bulwarks that he spoke.

'Hide me,' he cried hoarsely.

They gathered round him; all eyes averted from the

thing that was coming aboard. They had no thought of fighting it. It was Fate.

Only when Hook was hidden from them did curiosity loosen the limbs of the boys so that they could rush to the ship's side to see the crocodile climbing it. Then they got the strangest surprise of this Night of Nights; for it was no crocodile that was coming to their aid. It was Peter.

He signed to them not to give vent to any cry of admiration that might rouse suspicion. Then he went on ticking.

15 'Hook or Me this Time'

Odd things happen to all of us on our way through life without our noticing for a time that they have happened. Thus, to take an instance, we suddenly discover that we have been deaf in one ear for we don't know how long, but, say, half an hour. Now such an experience had come that night to Peter. When last we saw him he was stealing across the island with one finger to his lips and his dagger at the ready. He had seen the crocodile pass by without noticing anything peculiar about it, but by and by he remembered that it had not been ticking. At first he thought this eerie, but soon he concluded rightly that the clock had run down.

Without giving a thought to what might be the feelings of a fellow-creature thus abruptly deprived of its closest companion, Peter at once considered how he could turn the catastrophe to his own use; and he decided to tick, so that wild beasts should believe he was the crocodile and let him pass unmolested. He ticked superbly, but with one unforeseen result. The crocodile was among those who heard the sound, and it followed him, though whether with the purpose of regaining what it had lost, or merely as a friend under the belief that it was again ticking itself, will never be certainly known, for, like all slaves to a fixed idea, it was a stupid beast.

Peter reached the shore without mishap, and went straight on; his legs encountering the water as if quite unaware that they had entered a new element. Thus many animals pass from land to water, but no other human of whom I know. As he swam he had but one thought: 'Hook or me this time.' He had ticked so long that he now went on ticking without knowing that he was doing it. Had he known he would have stopped, for to board the brig by the help of the tick, though an ingenious idea, had not occurred to him.

On the contrary, he thought he had scaled her side as noiseless as a mouse; and he was amazed to see the pirates cowering from him, with Hook in their midst as abject as if he had heard the crocodile.

The crocodile! No sooner did Peter remember it than he heard the ticking. At first he thought the sound did come from the crocodile, and he looked behind him swiftly. Then he realized that he was doing it himself, and in a flash he understood the situation. 'How clever of me,' he thought at once, and signed to the boys not to burst into applause.

It was at this moment that Ed Teynte the quartermaster emerged from the forecastle and came along the deck. Now, reader, time what happened by your watch. Peter struck true and deep. John clapped his hands on the ill-fated pirate's mouth to stifle the dying groan. He fell forward. Four boys caught him to prevent the thud. Peter gave the signal, and the carrion was cast overboard.

There was a splash, and then silence. How long has it taken?

'One!' (Slightly had begun to count.)

None too soon, Peter, every inch of him on tiptoe, vanished into the cabin; for more than one pirate was screwing up his courage to look round. They could hear each other's distressed breathing now, which showed them that the more terrible sound had passed.

'It's gone, captain,' Smee said, wiping his spectacles. 'All's still again.'

Slowly Hook let his head emerge from his ruff, and listened so intently that he could have caught the echo of the tick. There was not a sound, and he drew himself up firmly to his full height.

'Then here's to Johnny Plank,' he cried brazenly, hating the boys more than ever because they had seen him unbend. He broke into the villainous ditty:

> 'Yo ho, yo ho, the frisky plank,
>   You walks along it so,
> Till it goes down and you goes down
>   To Davy Jones below!'

To terrorize the prisoners the more, though with a certain loss of dignity, he danced along an imaginary plank, grimacing at them as he sang; and when he finished he cried, 'Do you want a touch of the cat before you walk the plank?'

At that they fell on their knees. 'No, no,' they cried so piteously that every pirate smiled.

'Fetch the cat, Jukes,' said Hook; 'it's in the cabin.'

The cabin! Peter was in the cabin! The children gazed at each other.

'Aye, aye,' said Jukes blithely, and he strode into the cabin. They followed him with their eyes; they scarce knew that Hook had resumed his song, his dogs joining in with him:

'Yo ho, yo ho, the scratching cat,
  Its tails are nine, you know,
  And when they're writ upon your back –'

What was the last line will never be known, for of a
sudden the song was stayed by a dreadful screech from
the cabin. It wailed through the ship, and died away.
Then was heard a crowing sound which was well understood by the boys, but to the pirates was almost more
eerie than the screech.

'What was that?' cried Hook.

'Two,' said Slightly solemnly.

The Italian Cecco hesitated for a moment and then
swung into the cabin. He tottered out, haggard.

'What's the matter with Bill Jukes, you dog?' hissed
Hook, towering over him.

'The matter wi' him is he's dead, stabbed,' replied
Cecco in a hollow voice.

'Bill Jukes dead!' cried the startled pirates.

'The cabin's as black as a pit,' Cecco said, almost
gibbering, 'but there is something terrible in there: the
thing you heard crowing.'

The exultation of the boys, the lowering looks of the
pirates, both were seen by Hook.

'Cecco,' he said in his most steely voice, 'go back and
fetch me out that doodle-doo.'

Cecco, bravest of the brave, cowered before his captain, crying, 'No, no': but Hook was purring to his claw.

'Did you say you would go, Cecco?' he said musingly.

Cecco went, first flinging up his arms despairingly.
There was no more singing, all listened now; and again
came a death-screech and again a crow.

No one spoke except Slightly. 'Three,' he said.

Hook rallied his dogs with a gesture. ' 'Sdeath and odds
fish,' he thundered, 'who is to bring me that doodle-
doo?'

'Wait till Cecco comes out,' growled Starkey, and the others took up the cry.

'I think I heard you volunteer, Starkey,' said Hook, purring again.

'No, by thunder!' Starkey cried.

'My hook thinks you did,' said Hook, crossing to him. 'I wonder if it would not be advisable, Starkey, to humour the hook?'

'I'll swing before I go in there,' replied Starkey doggedly, and again he had the support of the crew.

'Is it mutiny?' asked Hook more pleasantly than ever. 'Starkey's ring-leader.'

'Captain, mercy,' Starkey whimpered, all of a tremble now.

'Shake hands, Starkey,' said Hook, proffering his claw.

Starkey looked round for help, but all deserted him. As he backed Hook advanced, and now the red spark was in his eye. With a despairing scream the pirate leapt upon Long Tom and precipitated himself into the sea.

'Four,' said Slightly.

'And now,' Hook asked courteously, 'did any other gentleman say mutiny?' Seizing a lantern and raising his claw with a menacing gesture, 'I'll bring out that doodle-doo myself,' he said, and sped into the cabin.

'Five.' How Slightly longed to say it. He wetted his lips to be ready, but Hook came staggering out, without his lantern.

'Something blew out the light,' he said a little unsteadily.

'Something!' echoed Mullins.

'What of Cecco?' demanded Noodler.

'He's as dead as Jukes,' said Hook shortly.

His reluctance to return to the cabin impressed them all unfavourably, and the mutinous sounds again broke forth. All pirates are superstitious; and Cookson cried,

'They do say the surest sign of a ship's accurst is when there's one on board more than can be accounted for.'

'I've heard,' muttered Mullins, 'he always boards the pirate craft at last. Had he a tail, captain?'

'They say,' said another, looking viciously at Hook, 'that when he comes it's in the likeness of the wickedest man aboard.'

'Had he a hook, captain?' asked Cookson insolently; and one after another took up the cry, 'The ship's doomed.' At this the children could not resist raising a cheer. Hook had wellnigh forgotten his prisoners, but as he swung round on them now his face lit up again.

'Lads,' he cried to his crew, 'here's a notion. Open the cabin door and drive them in. Let them fight the doodle-doo for their lives. If they kill him, we're so much the better; if he kills them we're none the worse.'

For the last time his dogs admired Hook, and devotedly they did his bidding. The boys, pretending to struggle, were pushed into the cabin and the door was closed on them.

'Now, listen,' cried Hook, and all listened. But not one dared to face the door. Yes, one, Wendy, who all this time had been bound to the mast. It was for neither a scream nor a crow that she was watching; it was for the reappearance of Peter.

She had not long to wait. In the cabin he had found the thing for which he had gone in search: the key that would free the children of their manacles; and now they all stole forth, armed with such weapons as they could find. First signing to them to hide, Peter cut Wendy's bonds, and then nothing could have been easier for them all to fly off together; but one thing barred the way, an oath, 'Hook or me this time.' So when he had freed Wendy, he whispered to her to conceal herself with the others and himself took her place by the mast, her cloak around him so that he should pass for her. Then he took a great breath and crowed.

To the pirates it was a voice crying that all the boys lay slain in the cabin; and they were panic-stricken. Hook tried to hearten them; but like the dogs he had made them they showed him their fangs, and he knew that if he took his eyes off them now they would leap at him.

'Lads,' he said, ready to cajole or strike as need be, but never quailing for an instant, 'I've thought it out. There's a Jonah aboard.'

'Aye,' they snarled, 'a man wi' a hook.'

'No, lads, no, it's the girl. Never was luck on a pirate ship wi' a woman on board. We'll right the ship when she's gone.'

Some of them remembered that this had been a saying of Flint's. 'It's worth trying,' they said doubtfully.

'Fling the girl overboard,' cried Hook; and they made a rush at the figure in the cloak.

'There's none can save you now, missy,' Mullins hissed jeeringly.

'There's one,' replied the figure.

'Who's that?'

'Peter Pan the avenger!' came the terrible answer; and as he spoke Peter flung off his cloak. Then they all knew who 'twas that had been undoing them in the cabin, and twice Hook essayed to speak and twice he failed. In that frightful moment I think his fierce heart broke.

At last he cried, 'Cleave him to the brisket,' but without conviction.

'Down, boys, and at them,' Peter's voice rang out; and in another moment the clash of arms was resounding through the ship. Had the pirates kept together it is certain that they would have won; but the onset came when they were all unstrung, and they ran hither and thither, striking wildly, each thinking himself the last survivor of the crew. Man to man they were the stronger; but they fought on the defensive only, which enabled the boys to hunt in pairs and choose their quarry. Some of the miscreants leapt into the sea; others hid in dark recesses, where they were found by Slightly, who did not fight, but ran about with a lantern which he flashed in their faces, so that they were half blinded and fell an easy prey to the reeking swords of the other boys. There was little sound to be heard but the clang of weapons, an occasional screech or splash, and Slightly monotonously counting – five – six – seven – eight – nine – ten – eleven.

I think all were gone when a group of savage boys surrounded Hook, who seemed to have a charmed life, as he kept them at bay in that circle of fire. They had done for his dogs, but this man alone seemed to be a match for them all. Again and again they closed upon him, and again and again he hewed a clear space. He had lifted up one boy with his hook, and was using him as a buckler, when another, who had just passed his sword through Mullins, sprang into the fray.

'Put up your swords, boys,' cried the newcomer, 'this man is mine.'

Thus suddenly Hook found himself face to face with Peter. The others drew back and formed a ring round them.

For long the two enemies looked at one another; Hook shuddering slightly, and Peter with the strange smile upon his face.

'So, Pan,' said Hook at last, 'this is all your doing.'

'Aye, James Hook,' came the stern answer, 'it is all my doing.'

'Proud and insolent youth,' said Hook, 'prepare to meet thy doom.'

'Dark and sinister man,' Peter answered, 'have at thee.'

Without more words they fell to, and for a space there was no advantage to either blade. Peter was a superb swordsman, and parried with dazzling rapidity; ever and anon he followed up a feint with a lunge that got past his foe's defence, but his shorter reach stood him in ill stead, and he could not drive the steel home. Hook, scarcely his inferior in brilliancy, but not quite so nimble

in wrist play, forced him back by the weight of his onset, hoping suddenly to end all with a favourite thrust, taught him long ago by Barbecue at Rio; but to his astonishment he found this thrust turned aside again and again. Then he sought to close and give the quietus with his iron hook, which all this time had been pawing the air; but Peter doubled under it and, lunging fiercely, pierced him in the ribs. At sight of his own blood, whose peculiar colour, you remember, was offensive to him, the sword fell from Hook's hand, and he was at Peter's mercy.

'Now!' cried all the boys; but with a magnificent gesture Peter invited his opponent to pick up his sword. Hook did so instantly, but with a tragic feeling that Peter was showing good form.

Hitherto he had thought it was some fiend fighting him, but darker suspicions assailed him now.

'Pan, who and what art thou?' he cried huskily.

'I'm youth, I'm joy,' Peter answered at a venture, 'I'm a little bird that has broken out of the egg.'

This, of course, was nonsense; but it was proof to the unhappy Hook that Peter did not know in the least who or what he was, which is the very pinnacle of good form.

'To't again,' he cried despairingly.

He fought now like a human flail, and every sweep of that terrible sword would have severed in twain any man or boy who obstructed it; but Peter fluttered round him as if the very wind it made blew him out of the danger zone. And again and again he darted in and pricked.

Hook was fighting now without hope. That passionate breast no longer asked for life; but for one boon it craved: to see Peter bad form before it was cold for ever.

Abandoning the fight he rushed into the powder magazine and fired it.

'In two minutes,' he cried, 'the ship will be blown to pieces.'

Now, now, he thought, true form will show.

But Peter issued from the powder magazine with the shell in his hands, and calmly flung it overboard.

What sort of form was Hook himself showing? Misguided man though he was, we may be glad, without sympathizing with him, that in the end he was true to the traditions of his race. The other boys were flying around him now, flouting, scornful; and as he staggered about the deck striking up at them impotently, his mind was no longer with them; it was slouching in the playing fields of long ago, or being sent up for good, or watching the wall-game from a famous wall. And his shoes were right, and his waistcoat was right, and his tie was right, and his socks were right.

James Hook, thou not wholly unheroic figure, farewell.

For we have come to his last moment.

Seeing Peter slowly advancing upon him through the air with dagger poised, he sprang upon the bulwarks to cast himself into the sea. He did not know that the crocodile was waiting for him; for we purposely stopped the clock that this knowledge might be spared him: a little mark of respect from us at the end.

He had one last triumph, which I think we need not grudge him. As he stood on the bulwark looking over his shoulder at Peter gliding through the air, he invited him with a gesture to use his foot. It made Peter kick instead of stab.

At last Hook had got the boon for which he craved.

'Bad form,' he cried jeeringly, and went content to the crocodile.

Thus perished James Hook.

'Seventeen,' Slightly sang out; but he was not quite correct in his figures. Fifteen paid the penalty for their crimes that night; but two reached the shore; Starkey to be captured by the redskins, who made him nurse for all their papooses, a melancholy come-down for a pirate, and Smee, who henceforth wandered about the world in his spectacles, making a precarious living by saying he was the only man that James Hook had feared.

Wendy, of course, had stood by taking no part in the fight, though watching Peter with glistening eyes; but now that all was over she became prominent again. She praised them equally, and shuddered delightfully when Michael showed her the place where he had killed one; and then she took them into Hook's cabin and pointed to his watch which was hanging on a nail. It said, 'half past one'!

The lateness of the hour was almost the biggest thing of all. She got them to bed in the pirates' bunks pretty quickly, you may be sure; all but Peter, who strutted up and down on deck, until at last he fell asleep by the side of Long Tom. He had one of his dreams that night, and cried in his sleep for a long time, and Wendy held him tight.

16 The Return Home

By two bells that morning they were all stirring their stumps; for there was a big sea running; and Tootles, the bo'sun, was among them, with a rope's end in his hand and chewing tobacco. They all donned pirate clothes cut off at the knee, shaved smartly, and tumbled up, with the true nautical roll and hitching their trousers.

It need not be said who was the captain. Nibs and John were first and second mate. There was a woman aboard. The rest were tars before the mast, and lived in the fo'c'sle. Peter had already lashed himself to the wheel; but he piped all hands and delivered a short address to them; said he hoped that they would do their duty like gallant hearties, but that he knew they were the scum of Rio and the Gold Coast, and if they snapped at him he would tear them. His bluff strident words struck the note sailors understand, and they cheered him lustily. Then a few sharp orders were given, and they turned the ship round, and nosed her for the mainland.

Captain Pan calculated, after consulting the ship's chart, that if this weather lasted they should strike the Azores about the 21st of June, after which it would save time to fly.

Some of them wanted it to be an honest ship and others were in favour of keeping it a pirate; but the captain treated them as dogs, and they dared not express their wishes to him even in a round robin. Instant obedience was the only safe thing. Slightly got a dozen for looking perplexed when told to take soundings. The general feeling was that Peter was honest just now to lull Wendy's suspicions, but that there might be a change when the new suit was ready, which, against her will, she was making for him out of some of Hook's wickedest garments. It was afterwards whispered among them that on the first night he wore this suit he sat long in the cabin with Hook's cigar-holder in his mouth and one hand clenched, all but the forefinger, which he bent and held threateningly aloft like a hook.

Instead of watching the ship, however, we must now return to that desolate home from which three of our characters had taken heartless flight so long ago. It seems a shame to have neglected No. 14 all this time; and yet we may be sure that Mrs Darling does not blame us. If we had returned sooner to look with sorrowful sympathy at her, she would probably have cried, 'Don't be silly; what do I matter? Do go back and keep an eye on the children.' So long as mothers are like this their children will take advantage of them; and they may lay to that.

Even now we venture into that familiar nursery only because its lawful occupants are on their way home; we are merely hurrying on in advance of them to see that their beds are properly aired and that Mr and Mrs Darling do not go out for the evening. We are no more than servants. Why on earth should their beds be properly aired, seeing that they left them in such a thankless hurry? Would it not serve them jolly well right if they came back and found that their parents were spending the week-end in the country? It would be the moral lesson they have been in need of ever since we met them; but if we contrived things in this way Mrs Darling would never forgive us.

One thing I should like to do immensely, and that is to tell her, in the way authors have, that the children are coming back, that indeed they will be here on Thursday week. This would spoil so completely the surprise to which Wendy and John and Michael are looking forward. They have been planning it out on the ship: mother's rapture, father's shout of joy, Nana's leap through the air to embrace them first, when what they ought to be preparing for is a good hiding. How delicious to spoil it all by breaking the news in advance; so that when they enter grandly Mrs Darling may not even offer Wendy her mouth, and Mr Darling may exclaim pettishly, 'Dash it all, here are those boys again.' However, we should get no thanks even for this. We are beginning to know Mrs Darling by this time and may be sure that she would upbraid us for depriving the children of their little pleasure.

'But, my dear madam, it is ten days till Thursday week; so that by telling you what's what, we can save you ten days of unhappiness.'

'Yes, but at what a cost! By depriving the children of ten minutes of delight.'

'Oh, if you look at it in that way.'

'What other way is there in which to look at it?'

You see, the woman had no proper spirit. I had meant to say extraordinarily nice things about her; but I despise her, and not one of them will I say now. She does not really need to be told to have things ready, for they are ready. All the beds are aired, and she never leaves the house, and observe, the window is open. For all the use we are to her, we might go back to the ship. However, as we are here we may as well stay and look on. That is all we are, lookers-on. Nobody really wants us. So let us watch and say jaggy things, in the hope that some of them will hurt.

The only change to be seen in the night-nursery is that between nine and six the kennel is no longer there. When the children flew away, Mr Darling felt in his bones that all the blame was his for having chained Nana up, and that from first to last she had been wiser than he. Of course, as we have seen, he was quite a simple man; indeed he might have passed for a boy again if he had been able to take his baldness off; but he had also a noble sense of justice and a lion courage to do what seemed right to him; and having thought the matter out with anxious care after the flight of the children, he went down

on all fours and crawled into the kennel. To all Mrs
Darling's dear invitations to him to come out he replied
sadly but firmly:

'No, my own one, this is the place for me.'

In the bitterness of his remorse he swore that he would
never leave the kennel until his children came back. Of
course this was a pity; but whatever Mr Darling did he
had to do in excess; otherwise he soon gave up doing
it. And there never was a more humble man than the
once proud George Darling, as he sat in the kennel of an
evening talking with his wife of their children and all
their pretty ways.

Very touching was his deference to Nana. He would
not let her come into the kennel, but on all other matters
he followed her wishes implicitly.

Every morning the kennel was carried with Mr Darling in it to a cab, which conveyed him to his office, and he returned home in the same way at six. Something of the strength of character of the man will be seen if we remember how sensitive he was to the opinion of neighbours: this man whose every movement now attracted surprised attention. Inwardly he must have suffered torture; but he preserved a calm exterior even when the young criticized his little home, and he always lifted his hat courteously to any lady who looked inside.

It may have been quixotic, but it was magnificent. Soon the inward meaning of it leaked out, and the great heart of the public was touched. Crowds followed the cab, cheering it lustily; charming girls scaled it to get his autograph; interviews appeared in the better class of papers, and society invited him to dinner and added, 'Do come in the kennel.'

On that eventful Thursday week Mrs Darling was in the night-nursery awaiting George's return home: a very sad-eyed woman. Now that we look at her closely and remember the gaiety of her in the old days, all gone now just because she has lost her babes, I find I won't be able to say nasty things about her after all. If she was too fond of her rubbishy children she couldn't help it. Look at her in her chair, where she has fallen asleep. The corner of her mouth, where one looks first, is almost withered up. Her hand moves restlessly on her breast as if she had a pain there. Some like Peter best and some like Wendy best, but I like her best. Suppose, to make her happy, we whisper to her in her sleep that the brats are coming back.

They are really within two miles of the window now, and flying strong, but all we need whisper is that they are on the way. Let's.

It is a pity we did it, for she had started up, calling their names; and there is no one in the room but Nana.

'O Nana, I dreamt my dear ones had come back.'

Nana had filmy eyes, but all she could do was to put her paw gently on her mistress's lap; and they were sitting together thus when the kennel was brought back. As Mr Darling puts his head out of it to kiss his wife, we see that his face is more worn than of yore, but has a softer expression.

He gave his hat to Liza, who took it scornfully; for she had no imagination, and was quite incapable of understanding the motives of such a man. Outside, the crowd who had accompanied the cab home were still cheering, and he was naturally not unmoved.

'Listen to them,' he said; 'it is very gratifying.'

'Lot of little boys,' sneered Liza.

'There were several adults today,' he assured her with a faint flush; but when she tossed her head he had not a word of reproof for her. Social success had not spoilt him; it had made him sweeter. For some time he sat half out of the kennel, talking with Mrs Darling of this success, and pressing her hand reassuringly when she said she hoped his head would not be turned by it.

'But if I had been a weak man,' he said. 'Good heavens, if I had been a weak man!'

'And, George,' she said timidly, 'you are as full of remorse as ever, aren't you?'

'Full of remorse as ever, dearest! See my punishment: living in a kennel.'

'But it is punishment, isn't it, George? You are sure you are not enjoying it?'

'My love!'

You may be sure she begged his pardon; and then, feeling drowsy, he curled round in the kennel.

'Won't you play me to sleep,' he asked, 'on the

nursery piano?' and as she was crossing to the day-nursery he added thoughtlessly, 'And shut that window. I feel a draught.'

'O George, never ask me to do that. The window must always be left open for them, always, always.'

Now it was his turn to beg her pardon; and she went into the day-nursery and played, and soon he was asleep; and while he slept, Wendy and John and Michael flew into the room.

Oh no. We have written it so, because that was the charming arrangement planned by them before we left the ship; but something must have happened since then, for it is not they who have flown in, it is Peter and Tinker Bell.

Peter's first words tell all.

'Quick, Tink,' he whispered, 'close the window; bar it. That's right. Now you and I must get away by the door; and when Wendy comes she will think her mother has barred her out; and she will have to go back with me.'

Now I understand what had hitherto puzzled me, why when Peter had exterminated the pirates he did not return to the island and leave Tink to escort the children to the mainland. This trick had been in his head all the time.

Instead of feeling that he was behaving badly he danced with glee; then he peeped into the day-nursery to see who was playing. He whispered to Tink, 'It's Wendy's mother. She is a pretty lady, but not so pretty as my mother. Her mouth is full of thimbles, but not so full as my mother's was.'

Of course he knew nothing whatever about his mother; but he sometimes bragged about her.

He did not know the tune, which was 'Home, Sweet Home', but he knew it was saying, 'Come back, Wendy, Wendy, Wendy'; and he cried exultantly, 'You will never see Wendy again, lady, for the window is barred.'

He peeped in again to see why the music had stopped; and now he saw that Mrs Darling had laid her head on the box, and that two tears were sitting on her eyes.

'She wants me to unbar the window,' thought Peter, 'but I won't, not I.'

He peeped again, and the tears were still there, or another two had taken their place.

'She's awfully fond of Wendy,' he said to himself. He was angry with her now for not seeing why she could not have Wendy.

The reason was so simple: 'I'm fond of her too. We can't both have her, lady.'

But the lady would not make the best of it, and he was unhappy. He ceased to look at her, but even then she would not let go of him. He skipped about and made funny faces, but when he stopped it was just as if she were inside him, knocking.

'Oh, all right,' he said at last, and gulped. Then he unbarred the window. 'Come on, Tink,' he cried, with a frightful sneer at the laws of nature; 'we don't want any silly mothers'; and he flew away.

Thus Wendy and John and Michael found the window open for them after all, which of course was more than they deserved. They alighted on the floor, quite unashamed of themselves; and the youngest one had already forgotten his home.

'John,' he said, looking around him doubtfully, 'I think I have been here before.'

'Of course you have, you silly. There is your old bed.'

'So it is,' Michael said, but not with much conviction.

'I say,' cried John, 'the kennel!' and he dashed across to look into it.

'Perhaps Nana is inside it,' Wendy said.

But John whistled. 'Hallo,' he said, 'there's a man nside it.'

'It's father!' exclaimed Wendy.

'Let me see father,' Michael begged eagerly, and he took a good look. 'He is not so big as the pirate I killed,' he said with such frank disappointment that I am glad Mr Darling was asleep; it would have been sad if those had been the first words he heard his little Michael say.

Wendy and John had been taken aback somewhat at finding their father in the kennel.

'Surely,' said John, like one who has lost faith in his memory, 'he used not to sleep in the kennel?'

'John,' Wendy said falteringly, 'perhaps we don't remember the old life as well as we thought we did.'

A chill fell upon them; and serve them right.

'It is very careless of mother,' said that young scoundrel John, 'not to be here when we come back.'

It was then that Mrs Darling began playing again.

'It's mother!' cried Wendy, peeping.

'So it is!' said John.

'Then you are not really our mother, Wendy?' asked Michael, who was surely sleepy.

'Oh dear!' exclaimed Wendy, with her first real twinge of remorse, 'it is quite time we came back.'

'Let us creep in,' John suggested, 'and put our hands over her eyes.'

But Wendy, who saw that they must break the joyous news more gently, had a better plan.

'Let us all slip into our beds, and be there when she comes in, just as if we had never been away.'

And so when Mrs Darling went back to the night-nursery to see if her husband was asleep, all the beds were occupied. The children waited for her cry of joy, but it did not come. She saw them, but she did not believe they were there. You see, she saw them in their beds so often in her dreams that she thought this was just the dream hanging around her still.

She sat down in the chair by the fire, where in the old days she had nursed them.

They could not understand this, and a cold fear fell upon all the three of them.

'Mother!' Wendy cried.

'That's Wendy,' she said, but still she was sure it was the dream.

'Mother!'

'That's John,' she said.

'Mother!' cried Michael. He knew her now.

'That's Michael,' she said, and she stretched out her arms for the three little selfish children they would never envelop again. Yes, they did, they went round Wendy and John and Michael, who had slipped out of bed and run to her.

'George, George,' she cried when she could speak; and Mr Darling woke to share her bliss, and Nana came rushing in. There could not have been a lovelier sight; but there was none to see it except a strange boy who was staring in at the window. He had ecstasies innumerable that other children can never know; but he was looking through the window at the one joy from which he must be for ever barred.

17 When Wendy Grew Up

I hope you want to know what became of the other boys. They were waiting below to give Wendy time to explain about them; and when they had counted five hundred they went up. They went up by the stair, because they thought this would make a better impression. They stood in a row in front of Mrs Darling, with their hats off, and wishing they were not wearing their pirate clothes. They said nothing, but their eyes asked her to have them. They ought to have looked at Mr Darling also, but they forgot about him.

Of course Mrs Darling said at once that she would have them; but Mr Darling was curiously depressed, and they saw that he considered six a rather large number.

'I must say,' he said to Wendy, 'that you don't do things by halves,' a grudging remark which the twins thought was pointed at them.

The first twin was the proud one, and he asked, flushing, 'Do you think we should be too much of a handful, sir? Because if so we can go away.'

'Father!' Wendy cried, shocked; but still the cloud was on him. He knew he was behaving unworthily, but he could not help it.

'We could lie doubled up,' said Nibs.

'I always cut their hair myself,' said Wendy.

'George!' Mrs Darling exclaimed, pained to see her dear one showing himself in such an unfavourable light.

Then he burst into tears, and the truth came out. He was as glad to have them as she was, he said, but he thought they should have asked his consent as well as hers, instead of treating him as a cypher in his own house.

'I don't think he is a cypher,' Tootles cried instantly. 'Do you think he is a cypher, Curly?'

'No, I don't. Do you think he is a cypher, Slightly?'

'Rather not. Twin, what do you think?'

It turned out that not one of them thought him a cypher; and he was absurdly gratified, and said he would find space for them all in the drawing-room if they fitted in.

'We'll fit in, sir,' they assured him.

'Then follow the leader,' he cried gaily. 'Mind you, I am not sure that we have a drawing-room, but we pretend we have, and it's all the same. Hoop la!'

He went off dancing through the house, and they all cried 'Hoop la!' and danced after him, searching for the drawing-room; and I forget whether they found it, but at any rate they found corners, and they all fitted in.

As for Peter, he saw Wendy once again before he flew away. He did not exactly come to the window, but he brushed against it in passing, so that she could open it if she liked and call to him. That was what she did.

'Hallo, Wendy, good-bye,' he said.

'Oh dear, are you going away?'

'Yes.'

'You don't feel, Peter,' she said falteringly, 'that you would like to say anything to my parents about a very sweet subject?'

'No.'

'About me, Peter?'

'No.'

Mrs Darling came to the window, for at present she was keeping a sharp eye on Wendy. She told Peter that she had adopted all the other boys, and would like to adopt him also.

'Would you send me to school?' he inquired craftily.

'Yes.'

'And then to an office?'

'I suppose so.'

'Soon I should be a man?'

'Very soon.'

'I don't want to go to school and learn solemn things,' he told her passionately. 'I don't want to be a man. O Wendy's mother, if I was to wake up and feel there was a beard!'

'Peter!' said Wendy the comforter, 'I should love you in a beard'; and Mrs Darling stretched out her arms to him, but he repulsed her.

'Keep back, lady, no one is going to catch me and make me a man.'

'But where are you going to live?'

'With Tink in the house we built for Wendy. The fairies are to put it high up among the tree-tops where they sleep at nights.'

'How lovely,' cried Wendy so longingly that Mrs Darling tightened her grip.

'I thought all the fairies were dead,' Mrs Darling said.

'There are always a lot of young ones,' explained Wendy, who was now quite an authority, 'because you see when a new baby laughs for the first time a new fairy is born, and as there are always new babies there are always new fairies. They live in nests on the tops of trees; and the mauve ones are boys and the white ones are girls, and the blue ones are just little sillies who are not sure what they are.'

'I shall have such fun,' said Peter, with one eye on Wendy.

'It will be rather lonely in the evening,' she said, 'sitting by the fire.'

'I shall have Tink.'

'Tink can't go a twentieth part of the way round,' she reminded him a little tartly.

'Sneaky tell-tale!' Tink called out from somewhere round the corner.

'It doesn't matter,' Peter said.

'O Peter, you know it matters.'

'Well then, come with me to the little house.'

'May I, Mummy?'

'Certainly not. I have got you home again, and I mean to keep you.'

'But he does so need a mother.'

'So do you, my love.'

'Oh, all right,' Peter said, as if he had asked her from politeness merely; but Mrs Darling saw his mouth twitch, and she made this handsome offer: to let Wendy go to him for a week every year to do his spring cleaning. Wendy would have preferred a more permanent arrangement; and it seemed to her that spring would be long in coming; but this promise sent Peter away quite gay again. He had no sense of time, and was so full of adventures that all I have told you about him is only a halfpenny-worth of them. I suppose it was because Wendy knew this that her last words to him were these rather plaintive ones:

'You won't forget me, Peter, will you, before spring-cleaning time comes?'

Of course Peter promised; and then he flew away. He took Mrs Darling's kiss with him. The kiss that had been for no one else Peter took quite easily. Funny. But she seemed satisfied.

Of course all the boys went to school; and most of them got into Class III but Slightly was put first into Class IV and then into Class V. Class I is the top class. Before they had attended school a week they saw what goats they had been not to remain on the island; but it was too late now, and soon they settled down to being as ordinary as you or me or Jenkins minor. It is sad to have to say that the power to fly gradually left them. At first Nana tied their feet to the bedposts so that they should not fly away in the night; and one of their diversions by day was to pretend to fall off buses; but by and by they ceased to tug at their bonds in bed, and found that they hurt themselves when they let go of the bus. In time they could not even fly after their hats. Want of practice, they called it; but what it really meant was that they no longer believed.

Michael believed longer than the other boys, though they jeered at him; so he was with Wendy when Peter came for her at the end of the first year. She flew away with Peter in the frock she had woven from leaves and berries in the Neverland, and her one fear was that he might notice how short it had become; but he never noticed, he had so much to say about himself.

She had looked forward to thrilling talks with him about old times, but new adventures had crowded the old ones from his mind.

'Who is Captain Hook?' he asked with interest when she spoke of the arch enemy.

'Don't you remember,' she asked, amazed, 'how you killed him and saved all our lives?'

'I forget them after I kill them,' he replied carelessly.

When she expressed a doubtful hope that Tinker Bell would be glad to see her he said, 'Who is Tinker Bell?'

'O Peter,' she said, shocked; but even when she explained he could not remember.

'There are such a lot of them,' he said. 'I expect she is no more.'

I expect he was right, for fairies don't live long, but they are so little that a short time seems a good while to them.

Wendy was pained too to find that the past year was but as yesterday to Peter; it had seemed such a long year of waiting to her. But he was exactly as fascinating as ever, and they had a lovely spring cleaning in the little house on the tree-tops.

Next year he did not come to her. She waited in a new frock because the old one simply would not meet; but he never came.

'Perhaps he is ill,' Michael said.

'You know he is never ill.'

Michael came close to her and whispered, with a shiver,

'Perhaps there is no such person, Wendy!' and then Wendy would have cried if Michael had not been crying.

Peter came next spring cleaning; and the strange thing was that he never knew he had missed a year.

That was the last time the girl Wendy ever saw him. For a little longer she tried for his sake not to have growing pains; and she felt she was untrue to him when she got a prize for general knowledge. But the years came and went without bringing the careless boy; and when they met again Wendy was a married woman, and Peter was no more to her than a little dust in the box in which she had kept her toys. Wendy was grown up. You need not be sorry for her. She was one of the kind that likes to grow up. In the end she grew up of her own free will a day quicker than other girls.

All the boys were grown up and done for by this time; so it is scarcely worth while saying anything more about them. You may see the twins and Nibs and Curly any day going to an office, each carrying a little bag and an umbrella. Michael is an engine-driver. Slightly married a lady of title, and so he became a lord. You see that judge in a wig coming out at the iron door? That used to be Tootles. The bearded man who doesn't know any story to tell his children was once John.

Wendy was married in white with a pink sash. It is strange to think that Peter did not alight in the church and forbid the banns.

Years rolled on again, and Wendy had a daughter. This ought not to be written in ink but in a golden splash.

She was called Jane, and always had an odd inquiring look, as if from the moment she arrived on the mainland she wanted to ask questions. When she was old enough to ask them they were mostly about Peter Pan. She loved to hear of Peter, and Wendy told her all she could remember in the very nursery from which the famous flight had taken place. It was Jane's nursery now, for her father had bought it at the three per cents from Wendy's father, who was no longer fond of stairs. Mrs Darling was now dead and forgotten.

There were only two beds in the nursery now, Jane's and her nurse's; and there was no kennel, for Nana also had passed away. She died of old age, and at the end she had been rather difficult to get on with; being very firmly convinced that no one knew how to look after children except herself.

Once a week Jane's nurse had her evening off; and then it was Wendy's part to put Jane to bed. That was the time for stories. It was Jane's invention to raise the sheet over her mother's head and her own, thus making a tent and in the awful darkness to whisper:

'What do we see now?'

'I don't think I see anything tonight,' says Wendy, with a feeling that if Nana were here she would object to further conversation.

'Yes, you do,' says Jane, 'you see when you were a little girl.'

'That is a long time ago, sweetheart,' said Wendy. 'Ah me, how time flies!'

'Does it fly,' asks the artful child, 'the way you flew when you were a little girl?'

'The way I flew! Do you know, Jane, I sometimes wonder whether I ever did really fly.'

'Yes, you did.'

'The dear old days when I could fly!'

'Why can't you fly now, mother?'

'Because I am grown up, dearest. When people grow up they forget the way.'

'Why do they forget the way?'

'Because they are no longer gay and innocent and

heartless. It is only the gay and innocent and heartless who can fly.'

'What is the gay and innocent and heartless? I do wish I was gay and innocent and heartless.'

Or perhaps Wendy admits that she does see something. 'I do believe,' she says, 'that it is this nursery.'

'I do believe it is,' says Jane. 'Go on.'

They are now embarked on the great adventure of the night when Peter flew in looking for his shadow.

'The foolish fellow,' says Wendy, 'tried to stick it on with soap, and when he could not he cried, and that woke me, and I sewed it on for him.'

'You have missed a bit,' interrupts Jane, who now knows the story better than her mother. 'When you saw him sitting on the floor crying, what did you say?'

'I sat up in bed and I said, "Boy, why are you crying?"'

'Yes, that was it,' says Jane, with a big breath.

'And then he flew us all away to the Neverland and the fairies and the pirates and the redskins and the mermaids' lagoon, and the home under the ground, and the little house.'

'Yes! Which did you like best of all?'

'I think I liked the home under the ground best of all.'

'Yes, so do I. What was the last thing Peter ever said to you?'

'The last thing he ever said to me was, "Just always be waiting for me, and then some night you will hear me crowing."'

'Yes.'

'But, alas! he forgot all about me.' Wendy said it with a smile. She was as grown up as that.

'What did his crow sound like?' Jane asked one evening.

'It was like this,' Wendy said, trying to imitate Peter's crow.

'No, it wasn't,' Jane said gravely, 'it was like this;' and she did it ever so much better than her mother.

Wendy was a little startled. 'My darling, how can you know?'

'I often hear it when I am sleeping,' Jane said.

'Ah yes, many girls hear it when they are sleeping, but I was the only one who heard it awake.'

'Lucky you,' said Jane.

And then one night came the tragedy. It was the spring of the year, and the story had been told for the night, and Jane was now asleep in her bed. Wendy was sitting on the floor, very close to the fire, so as to see to darn, for there was no other light in the nursery; and while she sat darning she heard a crow. Then the window blew open as of old, and Peter dropped on the floor.

He was exactly the same as ever, and Wendy saw at once that he still had all his first teeth.

He was a little boy, and she was grown up. She huddled by the fire not daring to move, helpless and guilty, a big woman.

'Hallo, Wendy,' he said, not noticing any difference, for he was thinking chiefly of himself; and in the dim light her white dress might have been the night-gown in which he had seen her first.

'Hallo, Peter,' she replied faintly, squeezing herself as small as possible. Something inside her was crying, 'Woman, woman, let go of me.'

'Hallo, where is John?' he asked, suddenly missing the third bed.

'John is not here now,' she gasped.

'Is Michael asleep?' he asked, with a careless glance at Jane.

'Yes,' she answered; and now she felt that she was untrue to Jane as well as to Peter.

'That is not Michael,' she said quickly, lest a judgement should fall on her.

Peter looked. 'Hallo, is it a new one?'

'Yes.'

'Boy or girl?'

'Girl.'

Now surely he would understand; but not a bit of it.

'Peter,' she said, faltering, 'are you expecting me to fly away with you?'

'Of course, that is why I have come.' He added a little sternly, 'Have you forgotten that this is spring-cleaning time?'

She knew it was useless to say that he had let many spring-cleaning times pass.

'I can't come,' she said apologetically, 'I have forgotten how to fly.'

'I'll soon teach you again.'

'O Peter, don't waste the fairy dust on me.'

She had risen; and now at last a fear assailed him. 'What is it?' he cried, shrinking.

'I will turn up the light,' she said, 'and then you can see for yourself.'

For almost the only time in his life that I know of, Peter was afraid. 'Don't turn up the light,' he cried.

She let her hands play in the hair of the tragic boy. She was not a little girl heart-broken about him; she was a grown woman smiling at it all, but they were wet smiles.

Then she turned up the light, and Peter saw. He gave a cry of pain; and when the tall beautiful creature stooped to lift him in her arms he drew back sharply.

'What is it?' he cried again.

She had to tell him.

'I am old, Peter. I am ever so much more than twenty. I grew up long ago.'

'You promised not to!'

'I couldn't help it. I am a married woman, Peter.'

'No, you're not.'

'Yes, and the little girl in the bed is my baby.'

'No, she's not.'

But he supposed she was; and he took a step towards the sleeping child with his dagger upraised. Of course he did not strike. He sat down on the floor instead and sobbed; and Wendy did not know how to comfort him, though she could have done it so easily once. She was only a woman now, and she ran out of the room to try to think.

Peter continued to cry, and soon his sobs woke Jane. She sat up in bed and was interested at once.

'Boy,' she said, 'why are you crying?'

Peter rose and bowed to her, and she bowed to him from the bed.

'Hallo,' he said.

'Hallo,' said Jane.

'My name is Peter Pan,' he told her.

'Yes, I know.'

'I came back for my mother,' he explained, 'to take her to the Neverland.'

'Yes, I know,' Jane said, 'I've been waiting for you.'

When Wendy returned diffidently she found Peter sitting on the bedpost crowing gloriously, while Jane in her nighty was flying round the room in solemn ecstasy.

'She is my mother,' Peter explained; and Jane descended and stood by his side, with the look on her face that he liked to see on ladies when they gazed at him.

'He does so need a mother,' Jane said.

'Yes, I know,' Wendy admitted rather forlornly; 'no one knows it so well as I.'

'Good-bye,' said Peter to Wendy; and he rose in the air, and the shameless Jane rose with him; it was already her easiest way of moving about.

Wendy rushed to the window.

'No, no,' she cried.

'It is just for spring-cleaning time,' Jane said; 'he wants me always to do his spring cleaning.'

'If only I could go with you,' Wendy sighed.

'You see you can't fly,' said Jane.

Of course in the end Wendy let them fly away together. Our last glimpse of her shows her at the window, watching them receding into the sky until they were as small as stars.

As you look at Wendy you may see her hair becoming white, and her figure little again, for all this happened long ago. Jane is now a common grown-up with a daughter called Margaret; and every spring-cleaning time, except when he forgets, Peter comes for Margaret and takes her to the Neverland, where she tells him stories about himself, to which he listens eagerly. When Margaret grows up she will have a daughter, who is to be Peter's mother in turn; and thus it will go on, so long as children are gay and innocent and heartless.

Some other Puffins you might enjoy

THE LAND OF GREEN GINGER
Noel Langley

What happened after Aladdin married his princess and started to live happily ever after? This book tells the story of Aladdin's son, the noble Prince Abu Ali, whose only fault was that he was far too nice, and who was sent by the Genie of the Lamp to set free a magician from the spell which had turned him into a Button-Nosed Tortoise.

A delightful, witty book which will be enjoyed by romantics of every age, and especially good for family reading aloud.

STIG OF THE DUMP
Clive King

Barney is a solitary eight year old, given to wandering off by himself. One day he is lying on the edge of a disused chalk pit when he tumbles over, lands in a sort of cave and meets 'somebody with a lot of shaggy hair and two bright black eyes' – wearing a rabbit skin and speaking in grunts. He names him Stig, they learn to understand each other, and together they raid the rubbish dump at the bottom of the pit, improve Stig's cave dwelling, and enjoy a series of adventures that are sometimes wildly improbable and sometimes extremely practical. One day they discover how to make a chimney with a batch of old tin cans, another they rescue the family silver from burglars, and on another they capture an escaped leopard.

MARTIN PIPPIN IN THE DAISY-FIELD
Eleanor Farjeon

Six little girls were spinning the evening away in a daisy field and Martin came to send them to bed. Perhaps they belonged to a dream themselves or perhaps it was just the stories Martin told them and the songs he sang that were dreams. Nobody wants to go to sleep who is enjoying being awake, and this is a book of the last delights and happy enchantments that are squeezed from a midsummer day before a child really must go to sleep.

Eleanor Farjeon's riverside setting and all her tales about the Tantony Pig, Elsie Piddock who skipped in her sleep, and the Mermaid who was born in a winkle, are touched with the contented glow of perfect storytelling.

THE PRINCESS AND CURDIE
George MacDonald

This story begins about a year after Curdie, the miner's son, saved the princess Irene from being carried away by the goblins who lived under the earth in her father's kingdom. (You can read about that in *The Princess and the Goblin*.)

It looked as if the kingdom would run like clockwork once the goblins were gone, but a lot can happen in a year, and so it came about that Irene's great-great-grandmother summoned Curdie and sent him to the king's court, where a great task awaited him. Before he went she gave him the rare and magic gift of knowing the true nature of every person whose hand he grasped. The adventures of Curdie and the princess in the city are just as exciting as their earlier ones among the goblins. For readers of nine and over.

If you have enjoyed this book and would like to know about others, why not join the Puffin Club? You will get a badge, membership book, *Puffin Post* four times a year, and the right to enter all the competitions.

Write for an application form to:

> The Puffin Club Secretary
> Penguin Books Ltd
> Harmondsworth
> Middlesex